The
Strength
Anthology
Series

VOLUME 1

Supporting the

Snow Leopard Publishing

The Strength Anthology Series: Volume 1
Copyright © 2018

This book is a work of fiction. Names, characters, businesses, organizations, places, events and incidents either are the product of the author's imagination or are used fictitiously. Any resemblance to actual persons, living or dead, events, or locales is entirely coincidental.

For information contact :
Snow Leopard Publishing
http://www.snowleopardpublishing.com
email: info@snowleopardpublishing.com

ISBN: 978-1-94436163-1(paperback)

Cover Photo by Marc Estes ©2018

First Edition: July 2018

A Note From The Publisher

It is with great pleasure that Snow Leopard Publishing releases this, the first in an ongoing series of Charitable Anthologies, to help charities around the world while at the same time promoting the work of new and seasoned authors.

Each piece in these anthologies have been donated by the authors for our program so that maximum donations can be made to the charity each anthology is dedicated too. We are excited to include authors from the world over into our program and look forward to meeting many more in the days to come.

We encourage you to continue to purchase other anthologies in this series as a portion of every book sold goes directly to a charity. If you like the writing styles of some or all of our authors, we also encourage you to visit their personal sites listed after their stories and poems for further information as well as our Owl's Nest Bookstore at Snowleopardpublishing.com .

Thank you for taking the time to read this anthology and we hope it leaves you with a desire to check our more.

Marc Estes
Publisher

Table Of Contents

Preacher's Son
Elaine White

After six weeks, Chuck was finally ready.

Life had never been normal, but it had always been pleasant. Just short of happiness for more than one reason. In the last six weeks, Defiance had added another reason. One that, through all his years of watching people and trying to figure them out, still didn't make sense.

So, he was going to find sense wherever it may fall.

He didn't think Defiance was a bully. For all that he'd made Chuck's last few weeks miserable, he wasn't a mean spirited person, cruel or physical in the way other bullies had been, even in a school with a Zero Tolerance policy. No, Defiance was misinformed, perhaps, or prone to judging people based on what he could see.

Chuck wasn't the same. At least, he hoped he wasn't.

Being the preacher's son, it was hard to tell what was his true personality sometimes, and what was learned behaviour from his father. Now, it was time to prove to himself and to Defiance that he was his own man.

As soon as the principal finished addressing the school assembly, she nodded to Chuck that it was his turn. And his choice. Taking a deep breath, he climbed the six steps up to the stage and stepped in front of the microphone that had been put there to amplify his naturally quiet voice.

He cleared his throat and looked out at the crowd. A few familiar faces smiled back at him, there was a head nod and a thumbs up of support from the few who knew what he was doing. He used that support to bolster his belief that this was the right thing to do.

"I've asked the principal if I can address you today, for one reason. To explain what that is, I'd like to read this statement I prepared, so that I don't get tongue tied or flake out at the last minute," Chuck confessed, a titter of laughter escaping him, at the same time a few of the audience joined him.

When the sound died down, he forged ahead.

"God says: don't cheat, don't lie, don't kill, don't be prideful.

Most parents who watch you live a life under those rules would say: I'm proud of you.

But the truth is that, without those things, you can't lie even to save someone's feelings. Marriages and school systems would fall apart if cheaters were never forgiven. If you can't have sex out of wedlock, girls or boys who are raped are considered sinners even though it wasn't their fault or choice. Girls who get pregnant from rape are told to commit murder, to abort their baby, so that they don't have a baby out of wedlock and 'shame' their families. Others are told to have that baby out of wedlock regardless, because they're good religious girls and don't want to commit murder.

Their choice is sin or sin.

There is no room in religion for consequences, compassion or logic, if you obey every rule in the Bible without pause. The Bible was written as a guideline, in a time when things were different.

I believe it has no standing in telling us how to live our lives today, unless we read each rule, law and guideline with the sense and logic of our time. People can still be religious while mixing denim and cotton. People can still be devout if they had sex in Bible study camp. Anyone with faith can have doubts, can have pride in their work and lie to protect those they love.

I believe that you can be a religious man if you have an open mind.

But I don't believe that you should preach the words of the Bible – don't lie, don't sin, don't let pride into your heart – if you can't also follow the teachings not spelled out for us: forgiveness, understanding and acceptance of all.

I choose a different path.

I choose not to follow religion, because no one on Earth can tell me which aspect of religion to follow. Do I have compassion and offer forgiveness, while never being prideful, boastful or lying? Or can I only follow the laws that are written?

I was raised to embrace and love all, according to the Bible. To be accepting and love thy neighbour. But life tells me that I'm wrong. That acceptance isn't deserved by those who are different. By those who aren't devout, aren't Christian, aren't straight or white or able bodied. Yet God and Jesus loved those people as much as They loved everyone else.

How can I, in good faith, trust a religion that lies to me?

My own father would disown me, try to change me, think me sinful, just because of who I am. Because of who I was born to be. Because of how God made me.

My name is Chuck and I'm gay."

The hall fell silent, as he ended his statement. Chuck was close to crying, but he kept his head down for a moment, thinking about the weight that had been lifted off his shoulders by confessing those things.

Out of the silence, one person clapped.

Chuck raised his head to find Harrison standing from his seat, clapping for him. Sterling and Freddy joined him, the latter boy whistling his approval. Within seconds, the entire LGBTTQQIAAP club, jokingly named the Bright Side Brigade, were on their feet, applauding his speech.

As foot stomps, whistling and shouting turned the hall into a concert of noise, Chuck let the tears fall. He only looked away when a hand fell on his shoulder.

"Wonderful job, Chuck. You were so brave," the principal said, with a gentle smile. He was given a nod of permission to leave the stage and took it quickly.

Skipping down the steps, he headed for the place where his friends were celebrating what the principal had called bravery. It wasn't brave or courageous. It was time. Time that he stood up to his father and Defiance, who misunderstood him. Time that he stepped out of the shadows and accepted his place in life.

As a young, gay man, who was struggling with his religion.

The club members had been so supportive of him, for months now, as he spilled his secrets to them and watched them hold them closely guarded. He had talked so often of his father's words and sermons being personal to him, a judgement of his own son, and how wrong it felt. Over time, they had started to attend church with him, so that he wasn't alone.

It was their courage that had inspired Chuck to do this. To finally speak up.

"Chuck," a voice called from a short distance away.

He stopped when he saw Defiance walking towards him. As though aware of how unsure Chuck was, he removed his hands from his pockets and showed that they were empty. "I'm sorry," he said quietly, stepping up close to say the rest, "I'm gay too. Your dad has been spending months making my life hell, at church. I'm sorry I took it out on you."

With a sigh, he realised the horrible truth. The sermons that were meant to teach Chuck to stay hidden in the closet, to convince him that his life was a sin and that he should marry a woman and have children, had resonated with others. They had made Defiance feel judged by his own preacher.

"I'm sorry my father can't see that we're the way we are because God made us that way. And I'm sorry that the God I once believed in lets these things happen to good, honest people like us," Chuck apologised, in return. He placed his hand on Defiance's arm, offered him a smile to show there were no hard feelings, and turned to walk away.

"That took real guts," he said, moving into step with him, "and...I don't have any right to ask...but can I drive you home?"

He wanted to laugh, as he realised what was happening. Looking up at Defiance, he realised he was being asked on a date. "I'd like that," he agreed, having always thought Defiance was a lovely person.

As they walked together, heading for the boisterous Bright Side Brigade waiting for him, Chuck realised that his so called bravery had just been eclipsed. By hope.

With a smile, he clasped Defiance's hand and watched a smile bloom on his usually sad face. It was quite wonderful how a smile could change a person. This one lit up the entire world.

The End

~

Author's Note

If you'd like to read more about the school Chuck attends, and the other members of the LGBTTQQIAAP club, you can find them in the upcoming short story collection, The Bright Side Brigade, by Elaine White.

~

About the Author

Elaine White is the author of multi-genre romance, covering everything from paranormal, crime and contemporary. Growing up in a small town and fighting cancer in her early teens taught her that life is short and dreams should be pursued. Living vicariously through her independent, and often hellion characters, she lives comfortably at home with a pack of wolves cleverly disguised as one standard poodle.

The Winner of two Watty Awards – Collector's Dream (An Unpredictable Life) and Hidden Gem (Faithfully) – and an Honourable

Mention in 2016's Rainbow Awards (A Royal Craving) she has explored the worlds of multiple genres but remains a romantic at heart. A self-professed geek, Elaine has fallen in love with reading and writing LGBT romance, offering diversity in both genre and character within her stories.

Black Candle

Jason Plouffe

"Wanna hangout?"

She was his type. Five five. A little stocky in the legs and shoulders. Blond hair extending from the hood of her parka. Under twenty-five.

"I'm heading home."

"C'mon, it's cold out here." She leaned into the wall and flashed her nice teeth. "Let's hangout."

Paul reached into his hood to stroke his hair, found air and stubbly skin. He still wasn't used to it. "I gotta get home."

"Can I come? I'm really cold."

"I've got roommates."

"Oh." She studied the ground with a disappointed pout. "Well, I know a place near here."

"Oh yeah?"

Paul glanced down the empty street. It was late. Early, really. The bars had been closed for hours.

"You got twenty bucks?"

"Ya."

"Ok. This way."

She started down the sidewalk, looked back to make sure he was follow-ing. "C'mon."

"What's your name?"

"Chelsea."

Paul stuffed his gloved hands into his pockets and flexed his fingers. "Hi."

"You're a nice guy, right?"

"I'm pretty chill."

"Sorry, it's just… it can be dangerous out here."

"Did they find any of those girls?"

"Not yet."

"That's scary."

"Scary for who? I know some of those girls."

"I can't imagine what that feels like."

"You don't have to." She slowed her stride and glanced at him hesitantly. "Sorry. It's just.. I'm scared."

The pull of Paul's groin grew more insistent. "I just want some fun. I'm safe."

"You seem pretty chill."

"Hopefully they catch him soon."

"Ya. Hopefully."

Chelsea stopped at the mouth of an alley.

"In here, but we have to be quiet."

The alley was dark. An old van was parked at the end. Steam belched from a sewer grate. No ground floor windows. Great place for a date.

"You wanna blowjob?"

"That sounds nice."

"You got twenty bucks, right?"

"Not 'til after."

"Can't you pay me now?"

"No. I've been burned too many times."

"But you're a nice guy, right?"

"Don't worry."

Paul leaned against the van and unzipped as Chelsea sank to her knees.

"Tell me when you're gonna come, ok?"

The air was so much colder than her mouth. He watched her parka hood bob back and forth. His hands itched. Finally, he pulled away and reached into her hood. He found the smooth expanse of her throat and began to squeeze. Instead of panicking, Chelsea leaned forward, found him, and started again, with greater pressure. He squeezed tighter.

"Oh, Paul."

He felt a sharp pinch, yelped at the pain. The bitch had a needle in her hand. Dizzying oblivion descended swiftly.

He was naked, his head pounded and he didn't know where he was. His body resisted movement. There was a distant awareness of cold. Shades of darkness advanced and receded in his vision.

Eventually, a dark balloon floated into view. He watched it bob back and forth with abstract curiosity.

"Hi Paul! I like your new haircut!"

He struggled to bring the balloon into focus. Shadows rippled across its surface. Grudgingly, his eyes apprehended the image of a strange, hovering mask. It had the features of a face, but positioned all wrong. The forehead rose to a shallow, rounded peak above a flattened, tooth-ringed cyclopean eye. Two small mouths sank into a massive, bearded jaw. Bizarre, and absently unsettling. He noticed he was shivering.

Reason slowly caught up to vision. Not a mask. A face. Someone was behind him. Crouched. Staring. Upside down to his perspective. What the hell was going on? He fought to reorient the image, straining against currents of disassociated resistance. His eyes fixated on a wide smile flashing in the flickering light. Nice teeth.

"Did you like my disguise? I think you did. We have a mutual interest in subterfuge. Though really, we see what we look for, don't we?"

The floating head had short brown hair and a half familiar face. Inside Paul's fuzzy brain a scratchy slow-mo film of a smashing dish played in reverse. It was Chelsea's face, but rounder without the blond hair, minus the girlishness. The air of petulant vulnerability was gone, replaced with a menacing confidence. He wasn't even sure he was looking at a female. And those eyes, staring at him intently. He recognized their excitement.

The puzzle was complete, all the fragments reintegrated and bonded with rendered fear.

Paul tried to scream. His mouth was immediately stuffed with something dry and scratchy. He gagged. Bile scorched his throat, leaked from his nose.

"Don't worry about the wig, Honey. I've got plenty."

Fear-laced adrenaline surged. Paul attempted to gain his bearings. Squinting, he determined he was in the back of a cargo van. Pale light shone from squat black candles placed at his armpits and between his splayed legs. He made a sluggish attempt to escape, and realized his limbs were tied to brackets attached to the walls. His helplessness sent muted waves of terror through his drugged body. He kept losing focus, returning to the image of the inhuman, floating mask. Like he'd been abducted by an alien.

"Paul, we need to talk. I've been looking all over for my friends. You know who I mean. Ashley. Ginger. Gem. I can't find them anywhere. But I found you."

Paul shuddered as once-was-Chelsea crawled across him and settled between his legs.

Shadows shifted as his captor lifted a fat black candle in front of a cheshire grin. The flame formed a trinity with the reflections shining in each eye. The undersides of lips and chin were cast into dark relief.

The candle titled as if it had a will of its own, splashing molten wax onto his exposed groin.

"Oops!"

Paul writhed in gagged agony.

"Oh, does pain turn you on, baby?"

Paul shut his eyes as burning droplets sprinkled his body.

"You know, Paul, you can learn a lot about someone from social media. For example, I know that you're a big comic book fan. Another mutual interest we share. I always dreamed of being a superhero. And you, you always dreamed of....Well, I think we know what your dreams are about."

His tormentor put down the candle and picked up a jagged shard of mirror, its edges stained with rust, or...Paul tore his gaze from the mirror, only to find those grim eyes.

"I guess we've both been turning our fantasies into realities, haven't we?"

Paul's horror took hold of his body as his captor gently ran the point of the mirror over his crotch. He was wracked by frantic, desperate spasms.

"One thing I never understood, though, was why so many of the heroes showed mercy to their enemies. You know what I mean? How could Batman just send the Joker to prison, knowing that he'd escape and kill again? It didn't make sense to me. I guess that's why I always liked the Punisher."

The makeshift blade caught the light of a candle, giving Paul a glimpse of his reflection. His naked, trussed body was graffitied with scrawling magic marker. The black text seemed to writhe across his body like bloodthirsty worms.

He thrashed on the floor of the van and attempted another futile scream.

It really was a great alley for a date. Noone disturbed them at all.

The end...for now.

Jason Plouffe is a hitchhiking, comic collecting costume enthusiast who grew up beside the Indian River in Douro, Ontario. He is a founding member of Knifehammer, a spandex thrash glam outfit from Peterborough, Ontario. Nomadic by nature, Jason currently maintains a base of operations in Downtown Toronto.

The Homecoming Apple
River Rivers

Hunter Hernandez entered the bathroom as Maria Maroni was leaving. The two tenth grade girls nearly collided. Hunter had startled Maria into dropping her unzipped makeup bag. The contents inside collided with the ceramic tile. They then exchanged a look of pure horror with one another. Without hesitation, Hunter was on her knees grabbing at the dirtied brushes, broken powder and scattered blotter papers. "Oh my god, my bad, I am so sorry!" she began to put away the rest into the bag, "please, don't kill me!"

"No promises," Her best efforts to apologize did nothing for the drama queen that was Maria, "Now give me back my stuff." As Hunter handed her the makeup back she noticed that the lipstick's coloring did not match what Maria currently wore. Her lips were peach, the lipstick was ruby red, belonging to someone else. Maria Maroni would never wear this shade. Her complexion was better suited for other tones. "Don't you think about kissing me, Hernandez. I'm not one of your volleyball teammates at a sleepover." The comment was a snide attack at her sexuality. She then shouldered past her.

Perhaps, Maria noticed Hunter looking at her lips and decided to take her chance at the insult. The rumor floating about Grimilde High was that Hunter Hernandez didn't like boys. It spread fast as she was this classes first almost lesbian. She didn't appreciate the gossip that took place when she wasn't around, however true the rumors might be.

Neither girl knew each other very well besides having some classes together. Maria Maroni, however, was notorious for having too high an opinion of herself. The boys in their shares classes often joked that her date to Homecoming should be a mirror. Hunter did her best to distance herself from people like Maria and her boyfriend Erin Prince. Luckily, they were in separate friend groups as Maria and Erin were Speech and Debate students and Hunter was an Archery and Track athlete

She went to the bathroom to wash her hands for lunch, Botany with Ms.Queen, left them crusted in the soil. Once inside Hunter noticed that written on the bathroom walls, stalls, and mirrors was a bold statement. Everywhere, displayed in bright red liquid lipstick it read, "Snow Weiss is the dumbest of them all." Taped to the most noticeable wall was Snow Weiss's grade from the Biology dissection test with Mr.Weiss. The honor student, athlete, and student body president received a D+ from her own father. Maria Maroni truly was a mirror. She meant to reflect and show Snow's grade to the world. The class watched during the live test as she failed to identify the heart and liver of a piglet, "It smells! The parts are squishy and too small and they all look the same!" She recalled Snow yelling out in frustration.

Hunter didn't want to feel laugh alongside the others. She liked the girl, the Weiss's were celebrated snowboarders and Snow, when eligible, would try out for the Olympics. She was talented enough too as her backyard was practically Mammoth Mountain. Even Mrs.Weiss was impressive, she had a Masters in Law and Sociology. The woman a renowned social justice activist for the inner city Fresno Community. Hunter's mom got along great with her as she was an environmentalist. When listening to them she learned something new everytime they talked.

This act was clearly Maria Maroni's attempt at revenge. Snow Weiss recently won more votes than Maria for class president. The focal point came during the final debate when Maria was asked by Snow, "What does a secretary-treasurer do?" It was a bold question as Erin Prince has secured the vote on the position due to dropout candidates. Maria answered with, "Find treasure?" By the end, she was nowhere in sight and didn't show up to school for a week. A rumor later floated around that Erin Prince was developing a crush on Snow Weiss and wanted to leave his girlfriend for her.

Hunter stared herself down through the lipstick on the mirror and came to a decision. She removed the rest from the mirror, tossing the ripped pieces into the trash. Then she took off her Fresno State hoodie and soaked it in the sink with some soap. The makeup would be hard to remove, she thought it unfair to have the nice old janitor cleanup after Maria's mess. The mirrors were the stingiest to scrub clean. She didn't have Windex and the water stained what she wiped clear. The stalls and walls were much easier to clean.

When on the very last bit of cleaning left, what Hunter feared the most happened. Another person walked in to witness Maria's revenge. This girl happened to be Snow Weiss herself. She stopped immediately, pulling out her earphones that were loudly playing 'Strangers' by Halsey, "Hunter? Did you write that?" she got closer and pointed to the roof, "This one calls me poisonous and a nasty word."

"I must've missed that one," Hunter finished wiping the lipstick stains left on the wall, "Listen, Snow, I didn't do this. I was the first to see, I thought I could get rid of it before anyone else walked in."

Snow Weiss was wearing an all-white sundress with matching sandals and purse. It made a nice contrast to her natural dark hair, eyes, and skin. When she arrived, the artificial lighting lit her up as if she were the only thing around. Her lipstick was red, the same color as the lettering Maria used, she figured it was stolen by her from Snow's belongings, "Here I am. Now deal with it. If you didn't do this, then who did?"

Hunter was no snitch, however, Maria Maroni's particular actions earned this, she would not fall on a sword for that girl, "The Mirror Maroni. She's after you." She climbed the sink to erase the nasty name above them. Snow even came over and let Hunter use her shoulder to balance and keep from falling, "Maria used your lipstick and posted your dissection grade. I tore that up." She informed her.

"Thank you, really, for doing all that," Snow Weiss crossed her arms and began to tap her feet, "This week has been rough. A lot has been happening with Homecoming nearby. The school's making me plan most of it, you know? It's stressful."

"Mhm, I bet. I have no sympathy for you there. You want into an Ivy league school, you must be willing accept these responsibilities." Hunter finished and got down. "Excuse me I need to wash my hands." She thought the dirt might never come off by how long she left it to dry on her skin. "So, you're a shoe-in for our Grimilde High Homecoming queen. Whoever is on your arm will be King. Any askers?"

Snow Weiss finally allowed herself to grin, it looked lovely on her, as did most the things she wore. She clearly wanted to focus on anything other than what Maria wrote, "Funny that you ask. Quite a few actually. Seven to be exact and I'm expecting at least one more this lunch period. They've been exhausting me. You think they could give a girl a break? I've taken to calling them the Seven Dorks."

Hunter suddenly remembered the first of Snow Weiss's homecoming suitors, Oscar Pierce, "Oh yeah! Didn't Oscar P-p-pierce ask while campaigning for you?" She asked while letting the air dryer roar into life, she spoke louder to be heard over it, "Someone told me he stuttered badly on his delivery and that his glasses fell off and broke. Did you let him down easy?"

"Yes, I did, he asked during the baking fundraiser. He made me and the school the sweetest smelling apple dumplings. Oscar's cute, stutter and all, we really shouldn't define him by that trait. He plans to get his doctorate in ophthalmology. Soon he'll be Doctor P-p-pierce." She covered her mouth and blushed redder than her lipstick, ashamed at her joke. "I might've said yes, though he's not quite my type. Anyways, I'm positive he's already found another date."

Hunter liked having Snow around to converse with. Lately, she only hung out with the guys and some female cousins who were much older than she. Her former best friend stopped hanging out with her once she privately confessed to her that she might like girls instead of boys, "Erin hasn't even asked Maria to homecoming yet. She's probably jealous of your Seven Dorks too. That girl loves to sabotage any happiness that isn't hers."

"You're right, I didn't think of it that way. She probably is afraid of losing Erin. From what his friends say he is trying to distance himself from her. They're excited about this development apparently. Worse than hens I tell you."

Hunter needed to put away her soaked hoodie, though she did not want the conversation to end, "Follow me to my locker and tell me more about these six other dorks."

"Gladly, we can get our lunches and spend the period in Ms.Queen's class."

The two girls who used to be close friends before high school had no trouble picking up their chemistry. They remembered year old inside jokes about each other. When one of them laughed the other just laughed even more Once they got their stuff Snow continued on about another boy who asked her out at the bake sale. Pinto the Grump arrived with fresh apple fritters too and a card to ask her out. When the Grump learned that he brought the same gift for Snow as Oscar, he accosted him. Screaming, "Why did you take my idea punk?" Pinto possessed severe anger issues. His face made it obvious, showing an overly large nose was broken in several places and his left eye was almost always black.

Snow was able to calm Pinto down by convincing him to instead come to the home-ec kitchens and bake a gooseberry pie for the sale.Snow was living for the opportunity to tell someone about these pathetic boys, "Then some days after them, Sterling showed portraits of me he drew. They were creepily accurate. Then in calligraphy was the homecoming question. He's known for sleeping during class, paying more attention to his notebook than the lectures, and rumor is it he's who vandalized Maria's glass coffin garden in the greenhouse. Of course, I turned him down."They passed the main hall where on the floor was a painting of a giant golden apple. It was their school symbol and their mascot was the Queen of Spades.

"After Sterling, the suitors just kept coming. Otis Mcdonald, our class clown with those big ears, was next. I attended the comedy show the theater kids put on. They were doing a mock homecoming, he pulled me on stage and asked me to homecoming. I said yes to keep the show fun. As soon as it ended he pulled me aside talking about what we were going to wear. That was an ordeal, let me tell you. Then the twins, Louis and Scotty Day, each showed up to my house at different dates to ask me. My parents were not happy about that. Richard showed up reeking like a farm from not showering and sneezing non-stop, it's no wonder he's always sick from school. Scotty was bashful as ever and gave me a charming letter. I'm going to take the time to respond, though I won't be going with him. The last to ask me was right here this morning. You must've missed it. Richard Happy showed up in a tuxedo with the school band behind him and performed a love song for me. I danced with him and enjoyed the song. It was tough saying no, he is a really positive person, brings out the best in people.."

"At this rate, you are running out of boys in our class to turn down." Hunter joked at her.

"Maybe I don't want a boy." Snow joked back.

Hunter led them into the classroom. The golden apple painted in the main hall reminded her to take out the apple from her lunch sack. She meant to give it Ms. Queen as a cliche gift, a tradition they've kept for a while. This golden apple came from a tree in the gardens the school kept, Hunter maintained this orchard for her botany project. The Golden Apple was known to symbolize trust. It was a way to gain favor with Ms. Queen since they were her favorite fruit. She waved hello to the teacher and set the apple on her desk.

Ms. Queen was busy grading papers and too distracted to pay much attention. Several students including the dorks Oscar, Louis, and Scotty were watching Erin and Maria argue. Maria was crying into paper towels, her makeup running badly. Erin Prince was frustrated and walked away from her. He collided with Snow, sending her directly into a bookshelf.

He somehow managed to catch her before she fell, "Did I frighten you? I'm so sorry." He asked as he made sure she was standing and not hurt. "This is awkward. I've actually been looking for you. I know it may seem odd and a bit rushed---Maria and I just broke up and I'm looking for a friend for this weekend. Please, wait for a second," Erin was acting oddly, he took off his royal blue jacket and put it around Snow. He then went to the teacher's desk to grab a sharpie and the golden apple Hunter bought for Ms. Queen. He wrote something on the apple and handed it snow, "The apple speaks for me. So, will you agree with what it says?"

Hunter had a good enough angle to read what the question on the apple, "Homecoming?" It boldly questioned Snow. Erin Prince was making it obvious he wanted to be Homecoming King and didn't think Maria was Queen material. At this moment the other's in the room crept closer to the action. All eyes were on Snow, all ear's patiently waiting for her answer.

What they got was the crisp chomp of an apple's first bite and some more chewing. When she finished swallowing her mouthful she answered him, "No I will not go with you Erin, but that's a really good tasting apple." Snow walked passed him and towards Hunter, to whom she handed the homecoming apple too, "I'm tired of being asked that question, I'll ask it instead. Hunter, the same question still applies. Will you?"

Her decision was clear once she bit into the apple too and nodded her head in agreement. Ms. Queen was the first to clap and the other reacted in vastly different manners. Some were supportive, some weren't. It didn't matter to them because they knew happily ever after could apply to them too. Hunter knew she and Snow would make the perfect Homecoming King and Queen.

Fairy Eye For The Squire Guy
River Rivers

It was 2018 and becoming harder to stay relevant as a Dark Lord in the United Empires of America. Grimstar knew this fact all too well. Ever since he peacefully rescinded his own empire and demilitarized his army the media just no longer cared. There were bigger and better news stories for them to report. *The Ice Zombie invasion in Canada for example...*

Grimstar and his undeadly appearance no longer inspired fear into the hearts of millions; T-shirts with his logo were sold in *Hot Topic* and American Eagle. Cartoons were made of his image to be sold. Children played with toys that looked like him and wore his face as a terrifying mask on Halloween. Even one of his first evil fortresses was now converted into a mini-mall.

The name Grimstar was mocked to his face and he regretfully went back to his birth name of Thomas Kline. His decline was an embarrassment that his Grim Ancestors would never have suffered. *No doubt they are looking down at me from the heavens with palms over their faces in embarrassment.* The Ancestors never ruled for less than a decade as he did (9 years and 6 months). These were the dark legends that built graveyards for the bones of heroes. They would've suffered torture before kneeling to *'Goodhearts'* as Grimstar chose to do. Those were the glory days Thomas only heard about in memory from his lava monster nanny. In his youth, he underestimated his Ancestor's accomplishments and overestimated his own.

His agent and publicist had plans to modernize his image and give him a new purpose in an ever-changing world. Evil Overlords were out of style. Black and white concepts were no longer tolerated by the masses. They want complication, grey morals, somebody who wasn't afraid to show their light and dark sides. This was clear when the voters elected a billionaire Troll for President instead of the Fae Godmother who was predicted to win. The Godmother was even supported by her nemesis, the One and Only Heroine. These plans started with an appearance on *Fairy Eye For The Squire Guy*. A show where a band of five diverse gays from the Empire reinvents a boring Lord's life.

This show might permanently make me a joke. Or it could give me a more accepted public image. He thought to himself.

Grimstar considered himself a progressive overlord. During his time in power, he allowed all creeds, races, and sexual identities to operate within his Genocide Militia. His main source of power was his necromancing, and the zombie horde he controlled via telepathy. The zombies and social outcasts got along. There was once an article about how his undead gas female chamber operator was married to the head nuclear weapons engineer who was very much alive. This was before those usurped his power even considered same-sex marriage as a possibility. And before living and undead marriage was legalized as well. Anyone could join Grimstar's forces as long as they too were determined to wipe out existence itself. Despite all that he'd never been around five gays at once. Let alone ten since the current show was a reboot and the members from the original show would be making an appearance for the 'Grimstar Special'. They would be his guests for an entire week. The upcoming event was making him a nervous wreck. He knew he wouldn't be ready when the cameras came.

The ten of them showed up to his Lair of Blood earlier than expected. It was morning and he still hadn't fed his Hydra it's four-horse breakfast. Apparently, they arrived at three am and were getting general shots and filming intros. His headless butler took care of it all and let him sleep, Crane was a professional. They interrupted him in the Doom Holdfast, a more fortified portion of the Castle Fortress. He was in his alchemist lab brewing a potion to kill some horses, to feed the Hydra when the ten fabulously dressed strangers interrupted his progress. Behind them followed the camera crew with an absurd amount of equipment. This group crammed into his tiny space and made themselves comfortable. Crane was in the background shrugging his shoulders like he tried to stop them.

Grimstar set down his mortar and pestle to glare at them suspiciously. An evil lord, even a dethroned one, must never greet anybody politely. More mistrust the better. There must always be a distance between the ruler and the ruled. He was surprised they even dared to approach him so closely. Grimstar, when his tyranny reigned, had a habit of killing those who brought him bad news. He would lose his temper and then--the messenger would be dead. He regretted each kill as loyal messengers were hard to come by.

The first guest who approached was a fairy with fabulous blonde hair, this glittery fellow obviously used a quality product, he ran his fingers through Grimstar's hair and immediately began to judge. "Hmm, alright, okay, I think I can work with this. Greasy, thin, tangled, we'll have to change all that of course. At least it's not dead yet. Scot, what do you think?" At this point, the fairy was using his wings to keep him off the ground to better view what he was working with.

Scot was a clean-cut leprechaun with gauges in his ears who had to climb onto a stool to properly examine, "He's got scalp burns."

"I was dropped into a volcano by our current the One and Only Heroine." Grimstar reminded them. "Peasant girl's don't mess around."

"Shh, baby, the professionals are talking." The fairy flipped his hair at him with some added sass.

Scot continued with his critiques, "Sparks, his hair offends me. It's dark and long like an emo singer. His pale arse skin doesn't help either. Has it ever seen sunlight? There are no nutrients to those roots. Where his hair parts at is so ugly I wanna barf, and that cowlick... I doubt he's changed his haircut since he was a sad little teenager torturing kittens in his bedroom." Scot then looked into Grimstar's eye's, into his soul. "Don't even get me started on your maniacal looking goatee. That's getting shaved."

"But, we can still save the look, right?"

Scot let out a heavy sigh, "We can try, we can try. . ."

"Speaking of saving. Your wardrobe needs a rescue too." A lanky limbed lizard person shoved himself between Sparks and Scot. "Zxelar, he's wearing a half-cape, I can smell the dust on it. His shoulders even have spikes, can you say tacky?"

Zxelar, the Grey Alien, stood in silence. Zxelar used to serve Grimstar until the fallout. This being wasn't actually a Grey Alien, he was a cosmic parasite that downloaded its brainwaves into a Grey's body. Zxelar spoke only when he was done looking. "Yes, the Old Master will need a modern wardrobe. If fear can evolve, he will too."

Then he recognized another thrall from his army. Grah was a Zombie staff sergeant who betrayed him when offered a California Dream House. Grah and the Merman were interior decorators with their own show. They were wasting no time in doing their job. New furniture was being moved in and his personal belongings were moved out. The pair paid Grimstar no mind and continued on with their duties.

A Slime Monster picked up a fresh batch of poison and took a big whiff that almost knocked him to the floor, "Whoo! What is that stuff? I didn't find anything like that in your spice cabinet? Hi, I'm Slyme, I do food and wine!"

The Warlock next had his face in his palm, "Lord Grimstar I apologize for my friend covering your workstation in green goo. That seems to be a fine batch of Sleep Hemlock you made. You are a master of your craft. As am I, when we are finished here you will be a food connoisseur." They then shook hands and the warlock gave him a slice of pegasus cheese to cry. The bite melted in his mouth the moment it touched his tongue. "No doubt you will find our service life-changing as that bite." There was something about his smile that Grimstar just didn't like. It was slimier than his friend Slyme.

The last two were a Centaur and Yeti who claimed to be experts in culture and lifestyle. Their names were Apple and Snow. They asked to speak to Grimstar alone in another room. Their conversation was mainly about reconnecting with his estranged daughter, finding faith again in his death-god religion, branding his CEO image to better reflect his growing tech company and to learn to be happy with the present by letting go of the past. All three were in tears as they were pouring their hearts out in front of the camera. Apple and Snow knew how to breach the walls he put up, instantly it felt like he'd known them for years. If these two were his advisors during the uprising he might never have lost to a plucky peasant girl. The three wiped their tears and enjoyed a group hug. Grimstar hadn't felt this emotional since they day he annihilated Chicago and his daughter rejected the throne's heirship.

That is in the past. I must move on, and move on he did, the show continued to film. The week with the ten gay men went faster than he expected. It wasn't fair, despite finding them exhausting to deal with at first, he now considered the group close friends. If his Evil Empire was still up and running he'd put each of them in valued positions. Each of them said this was their best episode yet. They even admitted they feared for their lives when passing over the river of damned souls via the drawbridge. At one point their fun got so chaotic they got him wear a speedo and streak across Orc training yard. It was funny because the Orc's were Republicans whose demographic largely voted for the Troll.

Sparks and Scot convinced him to shave his hair to a stubble and keep it short while allowing him to grow a handsome beard instead of a goatee. They even recognized Grimstar was a quarter vampire and took that into account when buying skincare products to account for the sun. They even took him to an eye doctor who figured out he was nearsighted and they purchased him glasses that helped and added an elegance to his makeover.

The Lizard Person and Zxelar completely revamped his wardrobe. They spent a few days just throwing away clothes and when they went shopping they told him no a lot more than he expected. Eventually, they settled on a class modern CEO look. His closet now contained blazers and suit jackets. With open dress shirts with designer labels and only the best fitting and in style pants. His shoes now we're only Gucci leather boots with belts to match. They said this brand new look would give him the confidence to conquer the boardroom instead of the nation-states.

The Warlock perfected some of Grimstar's family recipes and personal poisons while teaching him a dozen different methods to cook horses for his hydra. His information was beyond useful, but he still had a creepy demeanor to him. Slyme was all about eating natural and circadian biology. Basically, he wanted the dark lord to eat only from local resources where the sunlight he was living in was growing the food he ate. He instructed the undead cooks and farmers on different methods to keep this diet a possibility. The food didn't taste any better, though it did improve his physical well being.

With all these improvements he began to stand a little taller, sit a little straighter. Apple and Snow were quick to point that out. During the finale where he showed off the new and improved Grimstar, they surprised him with his daughter. It was a teary-eyed reunion with a lot of hugs and "I love you's" and "no, I love you's". They even showed her the blueprints to his company's next project that would use exoskeleton technology to turn the dragon into a starship capable of transporting people into space, possibly to Mars.

His daughter Evenstar was most impressed with the achievements of Grah and the Merman. She'd supported the zombie and his interior decorating passion since day one. They transformed a drab castle into a home a teenager could feel comfortable inviting people over to hang out in.

The details and work put in were insane. They installed a pool and hot-tub where the death pits were. A bar in was put in place of the gas chambers. His dungeon was turned into a man cave with movie theaters and bowling alleys. They updated the Undead armies uniforms to look less like some kind of 'Nazi Stormtrooper' and more like modern security. Upon the Merman's request, they demolished the secret passages and abandoned tunnels used by his arch nemesis to defeat him. *The fab ten got me flossin' now. I feel like my old ancestor the day he unleashed the black plague upon Europe. Just elated. If the world ended right now and I wasn't responsible I would be fine with that.*

After the filmed goodbye for the episodes ending, the original and rebooted cast stuck around to eat a dinner made by the Warlock and Slyme. The meal was lobster boiled alive in radioactive water to give it a specific flavoring. Slyme made this. The Warlock brought in wooden casks of wine crafted from his personal vineyards. He served Grimstar's family and Crane with a *'smooth'* white wine. He served the original cast a *'tart and sour'* green wine. He served the rebooted cast a *'deadly sweet'* red wine. The entire group of people toasted to the show's success and swallowed their drinks. Grimstar was the first to eat some lobster and complemented Slyme on his artistry.

That's when the Warlock slammed his empty drink onto the table, shattering the glass stand. He crushed the rest of the cup in his hand, ignoring the blood and injuries. Immediately the good vibes in the room ended. *"Sure, whatever, the lobster tasted delicious, but what about my wine? Grimstar I haven't heard a compliment about my art?"*

Grimstar pushed his chair back and stood to confront this wannabe wizard, "The wine was decent. I've had better. I prefer red wine over white, you should've served me that."

The Warlock stood too. His glare locked on the dark lord. "You're right. I should've served you the red wine." The dinner mates around them started dropping like flies. Specifically, those who had drank the red wine, the rebooted cast members. The Warlocks slimy smile oozed with satisfaction. "A reboot was a bad idea when the OG crew still breathes. This new show was a cash out without our approval. The money is ours, not theirs."

The original members pushed in their chairs to stand behind the warlock with their approval. Sparks tossed a used napkin Scot who was going into shock on the floor. Zxelar stood in silence as the Lizard Person struggled with dying, changing from its true form to the Queen of England, and back again. Grah kicked wiped the bile from the Merman's mouth and kicked him off his chair. Snow laughed and told Grimstar he could feed the Apple the Centaur to his Hydra with those cooking methods he learned. Warlock stayed focused on Grimstar and paid no mind to Slyme who was an unrecognizable puddle of goop at this point.

They're all dead. My friends killed my friends.

The Warlock continued to speak, "They voted for the Orc to be our President. All five of them. They betrayed their own kind. In this new world, we can't have that. Our idea is that we have you run against the Troll next election. Everybody loves a redemption story. With your rising popularity, you can easily win. We will help you make your Dragon Starship to a reality. Thanks to us and our inside connections you will rule the people who once cast you down. How sweet does that taste."

Grimstar bit his tongue in stress, all this information was too much to handle at once, he'd killed messengers for less. "All that power? Yes, that would be sweet. What would I have to give? Someone has to take the blame for these murders."

The Warlock broke his smile to laugh at him, he placed his hand on his hips, the first time he came off feminine, "As if we haven't thought of that. Have Crane reach into Scot's suit pocket."

Crane was hesitant, but when Grimstar nodded his head yes, he reached inside and pulled out an envelope and letter, "A suicide note." He explained. "Scot's hand is forged with accuracy and it explains how since his husband left him he couldn't handle being alone. He resented his friend's successes and relationships and wanted to take them out with him. He stole 'Sleepy Hemlock' from Grimstar's storage and put in the wine cask when Warlock wasn't looking."

Snow reached out with his hand out, speaking for the group. "What do you say future President Grimstar, will you agree to our plan?"

Grimstar refused the handshake, he walked over and took a sip of the red wine. He was immune to the poison inside. He handed the glass to the Warlock, "I'll agree only if the Warlock drinks the poison and kills himself too. He's been close friends with Scot for years. That's a hole in his facade. I can't trust a man like him."

Sparks spoke out for the Warlock, the other four were too shocked to speak. "Whoa there! Isn't that a little too *harsh?*"

"No, it's not. Else I'll order my troops in to flay you all alive as the alternative. Grah can attest to that. It's his life or yours. I am an evil lord after all."

The Warlocks smiled died. He wasted no words and ran for the door. Snow the Yeti grabbed ahold of him. Grimstar's daughter Evenstar helped too by holding the man's hands behind his back. The rest fell in line as Snow was the strongest. Grimstar got close to him and put the wine to his lips, "Two betrayals in one night. Drink up Warlock, the wine is ***deadly sweet.***"

About The Author

River Rivers is a writer lost in the Cascadian mountain lands of Oregon. He spends his time with his two adopted Pitbulls, Gemma and Murphy. Somehow in between their chaos, he finds a time for work and fiction. His most recent stories are currently featured on Literally Stories, Who Writes Short Shorts, TallTaleTv, Snow Leopard Publishing and the Drabble Dark Anthology.

You can follow River Rivers on Twitter https://twitter.com/Catch22Fiction

FELIS CATUS BIONICUS:
-PUBLISHED IN MARCH https://literallystories2014.com/2018/03/23/felis-catus-bionicus-by-river-rivers/
-PUBLISHED IN MAY NARRATED
https://www.youtube.com/channel/UCDDvUcNa5_hDQJ1-jWSJF4Q

-DINNER STAINS: https://whowritesshortshorts.com/

The Message of My Elders

Candace Merideth

The porridge seeps from the bowl my grandmother used to say. I wondered if the porridge was like honey, nearing the porcelain dish like a slowly oozing fountain, or watery – an avalanche bursting forward in some momentum explained by physics. When my grandmother died a little blue bird flew through the window and landed on the church pew across from me and ruffed up its wings, howling with a subtle tweet before darting off over the chest of my grandmother and landing once again, this time on the branches beside a rosary.

In the weeks that ensued the neighbors, family and friends talked about my grandmother's infidelity; they talked about how she posed in her bra and panties for an artist who drew her in an image they had not seen – they always said she was lovely but deserved to be shunned by them. It was the artist, according to the legend of my grandmother, who wooed her into a relationship that was not my grandfather. They divorced early in the year 1967 and my mother was pregnant at the age of twenty. My grandmother's husband, my mom's step dad, was an artist whose landscapes adorned the walls; he would tell me stories about how God made the weather – his tears rained from Heaven.

It was upon his death when the neighbors talked about his exquisite art – how skillful he was in creating the masterpiece that still hangs on the wall in the local church. They said she just didn't have talents to compare but my grandmother taught me every stitch that strings together my own daughter's nursery blanket. My grandfather, my mother's father, used to take me on pony rides and told me once if you wish upon the red bird (the Cardinal) that God would be listening and my wish would come true. The town said my grandfather was too broken to ever be mended but it was he who fixed their carburetor or an axle of some diesel engine.

On the day of my grandmother's death my grandfather etched her image that radiates from her headstone in the light of angels made of glass, and it was my grandfather who said she was an angel that he couldn't love her enough – that he never showed her compassion, the way he did finally, with me. The town said his grievances were her duty to mend but he always said that love is to be shown through compassion, understanding and even sympathy; it was my grandmother who said he was always a man of his word – he did change, as he said he would, if not for her but for another. She died before my grandmother and her love was thick – and extended to the children that were not her own; the town said how she was too much the rebel, but it was she who taught me the strength to keep going past the blood, the sweat and the tears to become more than a medical student – but a great mother to a little girl who always said her grandmother gives her the best hugs.

The town didn't know but the porridge always seeps from the bowl as my grandmother said, and that little blue bird took with it the messages of my elders.

Jillian

Candace Meredith

I stopped my car from hitting her body. She laid sprawled out on her back with her smashed vehicle gone over the median. I maneuvered left and blocked an entire three lanes of oncoming traffic – *please don't hit her body* I prayed. It was an automatic response – turning the vehicle and being smashed on the driver side with my legs suspended beneath the console and glass cut my face. I didn't see her leave her body – there was no evidence of an ascension but I twisted my upper body so I could see her face – see if her eyes gave any sense of life and that's when it happened; she was sitting right there beside me in my once vacant passenger seat with her eyes emanating like a flash of gold.

"But you were out there," I said smoothly, still obviously dumbfounded.

"It's okay," she said and placed her left hand to my right knee and that's when I noticed it; there was blood draining from a hole in my hip – but she looked flawless. Her skin was olive and her eyes, a stunning green peering behind thick, black framed glasses (they were undamaged) and then I became more curious; how did she survive unscathed? I saw, as she swerved, her small black Jetta turned on its side and she was ejected from the vehicle – she avoided hitting me head on when she diverted over the median.

"Everything will be okay," she said, breaking my concentration. "They will be here soon." She continued and her left hand squeezed harder on my right knee so that the blood flow (or more correctly, blood loss) would lessen so. I had an inkling to ask her name but I remained stunned.

"It's Jillian." She said – was she reading my mind?

"My names Jarrod," I responded.

"I know," she said, and smiled so radiantly from her dazzling façade. "What you did was very brave," she continued, and I thought I started to see a tear in her eye but the world became a haze, a dream-like fog, and that's when I saw it again – there were lights and I was on a trolly, strolling through the sterile hallway and I began yelling for Jillian – a woman whom I didn't know then there she was again, back in the car, "how did I get here?" I said and she parted her lips, "you have come by ambulance," she nodded, and out my window I could see them; the paramedics were surrounding her body – or where her body had been. And they swarmed my car in the haze and then I was in a room; the sterile surroundings of tubes and monitors.

"You have lost a lot of blood," a man said – a doctor? His white overcoat said so and I grimaced a weak smile, "but how is the young lady?" I asked while darting my eyes among the confusion.

"You did the best you could." He went on, "but you're bleeding internally and we must begin surgery."

"She held my hand," I said, trying to explain.

"They did all they could," he said when Jillian parted the cloth drapes and kissed me upon my forehead before walking away. Her entire physique was unscathed and she was beautifully enamored in gold. I learned that my angel died that night, but I had lived; she had saved me.

I never thought I was the one who needed saving – that is, until I got the letters from her children – *what do angels look like* they asked and I knew then, that only I could see her as she had once been.

Candace Meredith earned her Bachelor of Science degree in English Creative Writing from Frostburg State University in the spring of 2008. Her works of poetry, photography and fiction have appeared in literary journals Bittersweet, The Backbone Mountain Review, The Broadkill Review, In God's Hand/ Writers of Grace, Unlikely Stories Mark V online journal, Scryptic Magazine, Mojave River Press and Greensilk Journal.

Mary

Melisa Quigley

The day seemed like any other. The alarm clock buzzed, and I turned it off. I moved my right leg across my husband John's side of the bed. It was cold. He had already left for work on early shift. I wished it were the weekend, so I could stay in bed for a few minutes longer, but it was a weekday, so I got up. For the past three months, he had been working overtime. He said he wanted to take me on a holiday overseas. We hadn't been away since our honeymoon in Thailand where we spent seven days in Phuket with Mary. His wife died giving birth to her. I met John through a mutual friend when Mary was two. Three years later, he asked me to marry him. It seemed like we'd been saving forever to go to Fiji for our eleventh wedding anniversary, but bills had made us dip into our savings. We'd stayed home for our holidays. Palm trees, golden sandy beaches and sun-filled days at a tropical island resort were beyond my comprehension. This time it would be just the two of us. We hadn't told Mary our plans. She would be staying at her grandparents when the time came for us to go.

Mary's school lunch was still sitting in a brown paper bag on the bench where I'd left it John and I had found her harder to connect with since she'd started Year 11. According to Mary, we were dumb and didn't understand her. The three of us had more arguments lately. Mary had come home from her girlfriend's house and told us over dinner that she wanted to get a tattoo and dye her hair purple.

'You'll ruin your hair,' I said. 'It'll take ages to grow out.'

'But Amy's mum dyed Amy's hair purple.'

'No daughter of mine is getting a tattoo,' said John. 'You're too bloody young.'

'But Louise got a tattoo. It's really cool,' said Mary. She sulked and didn't talk to us for the rest of the week.

I drove a different way to work to drop her lunch off. The traffic was moving too slow for my liking A truck in front of me blocked my view, so I couldn't see what was happening up ahead. I glanced at my watch and sighed.

Damn you, Mary for leaving your sandwiches behind. Now I'll be late for work, I thought creeping forward. I turned the radio on, flicking from station to station to see if there was a traffic report but all I heard was morning banter from a radio host or music. No sooner had we started moving, and then we stopped again.

Further, down the road I came to a standstill. There was an accident near Mary's school. A paint truck was sitting on a slight angle in the other lane. A sea of white paint washed across the road. The ambulance's lights started to flash, and its siren came on. A police officer stood in the middle of the road, put his palm out and blew a whistle to stop the traffic so the ambulance could do a U-turn before moving the traffic on.

I pulled into a side street several blocks away and rang a work colleague on my cell phone to let them know I was running late. My boss had sacked two people last week and none of us knew why. I ran to Mary's high school, my new high heel shoes cutting into my feet. A headband like one Mary wore lay in the gutter.

Teenagers loitered in the street watching what was happening. Three girls were sitting on the steps talking near the entrance.

'I hope she's alright,' one said.

'She had her headphones in and wasn't watching,' said another.

'They don't know how injured she is,' said a girl to a boy walking past me.

I ran up the stairs to reception. 'My daughter, Mary Miller, forgot her sandwiches,' I said to the woman behind the desk.

'Would you like me to call her over the loudspeaker?'

'If you don't mind.' Why is it when you're in a hurry, things seem to take forever? My eyes searched the corridor for Mary, expecting her to appear when my cell phone rang.

'Where are you?' said my secretary Denise.

'Stuck in traffic. I rang Sylvia earlier to let her know. Why?'

'The meeting's about to start.'

'Tel them I won't be long.' I hung up.

'I'm sorry, I've got to go,' I said to the woman behind the desk. 'Mary's in Ms Sweeny's class, 11E. Can you make sure she gets them?' I handed her the bag. The woman took it and said nothing. There was no point embarrassing Mary anyway. No child likes to see their mum at school. How uncool would that be, especially when you're sixteen but act like you're twenty-four?

I sent her a text to let her know I'd left her sandwiches at reception, but she didn't reply.

When I arrived at work, the meeting hadn't started. A few other people arrived late because of the traffic so my boss had waited for me.

He asked me to stay after the meeting. 'Joan, I need you to come to a meeting with me now – in Coburg. It's that new client I was telling you about. They want us to analyse their business.'

'Sure,' I said breathing a sigh of relief. 'I'll just tell Denise.'

I went back to my office. 'I've got to leave now,' I said to her. 'Just take messages and I'll deal with them later.'

'What time will you be back?' she said.

'I don't know.'

When I arrived home John's car wasn't in the garage.

'Mary, I'm home,' I called when I opened the front door. The television wasn't on and her bedroom was how she'd always left it – in a mess.

I rang John on his cell phone to see how much longer he'd be. We never rang one another when we were at work. John didn't hear his phone in the factory because of the noise of the machinery and I was always in and out of meetings. His phone went to message bank.

'Hi John, it's me. Let me know when you're leaving.'

In the fridge was some leftover chicken casserole I'd made on the weekend, so I put it in the oven and set the table. Puss meowed at the back door and I let her inside and fed her.

The doorbell rang. A male and female police officer peered at me from the other side of the flywire, surprising me. The male officer took his hat off.

'Are you Mrs Miller?' he said.

'Yes.'

'May we come in?'

I unlocked the security door and they followed me into the living room. My mind was all over the place, wondering what they wanted. They sat side by side on the couch and I sat opposite them. Through the curtain, Mary walked up the driveway.

The back door clicked open and the three of us watched Mary walk into the kitchen opposite. I nodded to her to come into the room. She sat on the arm of the chair I was sitting on.

'Would you like to come with me?' The female police officer asked Mary.

'No, my daughter's staying here with me,' I said and clasped Mary's hand, wondering what she'd done wrong.

'There was an accident …' said the male police officer and coughed. His words floated in the air and disappeared.

It was at that moment I recalled the accident I'd seen earlier that morning. 'Yes, I saw it on the way to work.'

'I'm terribly sorry,' said the police officer. 'There was another accident – at your husband's work. We rang you at home, but there was no answer.

I went into the kitchen and picked up the landline phone which we hardly ever used, and it beeped. 'You have five new messages…' I hung up the phone. My mind went blank and I bit my bottom lip.

My voice sounded shrill yet raspy like someone else was speaking. 'But there has to be some mistake.'

'Mr Miller had a heart attack when he was driving a forklift at work. It crashed into a wall and he died instantly.'

Melisa Quigley is a writer and poet who has had her flash fiction, short stories and poetry published in several anthologies in Australia and America. She came second in the 2015 City of Glen Eira My Brother Jack Awards for her short story, The House on the Hill and commended for her poem, Ice Cream. She lives with her husband and two dogs in Australia and is currently writing her first novel.

Blog: https://melisaquigley.wordpress.com/

Twitter: @MQuigley1963

Reset
(Jerry Woke Up)
Kyt Wright

Jerry woke up feeling dreadful, he had really got trousered last night, his mouth felt as if a small rodent had been nesting in it and his head was POUNDING!

He staggered to the bathroom for his morning micturition then what Louise had said yesterday came back to him. 'Jerry please you have got to stop drinking so much!' he had ignored her and carried on sinking pints, at some point she had left glaring at him 'I've had enough, we're through Jerry' she had said, at least that's what he thought she had said, everything was a bit fuzzy by then.

He looked at the black eye remembered he'd left his mates and followed Louise outside promising to himself he would change then saw Louise in an embrace with Corin her smarmy friend from the office, *who just happened to be in the pub as well.*

'You bitch' he had snarled.

The bastard had sneered 'did you really think she liked you, you drunken loser?'

'Corin, leave it' said Louise sadly 'I'm sorry Jerry I gave you so many chances.' Corin had sneered again so Jerry swung at him knocking him backwards. 'No stop it!' Louise yelled grabbing his arm… He punched her without thinking.

'You fucking animal' Corin came angrily back at him…

Jerry touched the bruised eye. *I hit her, oh my god I hit Lou!*

'Don't you ever ever come near me again, I never want to see you again!' she had screamed as Corin led her off, his arm around her, mouth bloody.

He shaved and leaned on the sink deciding whether or not to throw up, he had surpassed himself this time *I wish the ground would swallow me up! Can't face work I'll phone in sick…* Jerry realised he couldn't, the bastard manager would guess he was hungover again and he was on his last warning, cleaning his teeth quickly spitting out blood, *this is getting worse* he watched the red goo as it swirled down the plughole.

Jerry glanced at his watch *Christ!* The bus was due in ten minutes, if he skipped breakfast he would catch it, *his car like his life was broken down at present.*

He quickly dragged the comb through his hair and winced as it caught on something, pulling his fringe back he could see something red and round just above his forehead, something red and round? He moved his head closer to the mirror then retched and this time was sick in the sink. There was a round red button on his head with something written on it. Feeling faint he stumbled into the front room and sat heavily on the settee.

Don't panic, you're having some kind of screwed up dream, calm down! Jerry waited till his rapid breathing slowed then gingerly felt his scalp. It was still there and it was stuck fast! The bus for work rattled past in the street below, *work could wait this was serious.* Louise had left an old compact in a sideboard drawer so he found it out and grimacing held it up to see the object on his head. He steeled himself to have a good look, it was a bright red button with RESET written upon it *backwards of course*, he sat back and tried to recall what had happened last night, *had one of his friends superglued it to him as a joke? No it seemed to be fixed into his skull. Aliens! They had abducted him and fitted it in their UFO, no that was stupid… but how did it get there?* He remembered bumbling home drunkenly wishing he hadn't been so stupid, then he had tripped and landed up against Mr Mandalia's shop window coming face to face with a picture of Lakshmi there. He once had a long conversation with his friend Kirit about the Hindu pantheon and remembered she was the goddess of money, wealth and fortune and in this case fortune meant luck.

Well Lakshmi if you're so lucky how about giving me some of it, I've really screwed my life up, I just would love to start all over again' he had thought…

He looked at the button in the mirror one more time, took a deep breath and pressed it.

Kyt Wright was born in the Lincolnshire in 1957 grew up reading Science Fiction and harboured an urge to write from his early teens creating a plethora of long essays that were read only by a few friends and his English teacher who gave him criticism and encouragement. Moving to Leicestershire in the 1970's Kyt became an Electronic Engineering apprentice then Draughtsman and married, two sons arrived shortly after but no books appeared…

December 2016 and the desire to write returned with a vengeance, a science fiction romance set in an alternate universe was brought into being based on an idea from his late teens and no less than three sequels lurk in the shadows. As yet Kyt remains an unpublished author but maintains a webpage which contains a great swathe of his doodles, thoughts and writings at :

https://kytwright.wordpress.com/

Searching

Kimberly Cunningham

It was the cold I remember the most. Seemed to cut through straight to my soul. No matter where I was that darn coldness seemed to follow me. Days were spent walking through the woods looking for survivors in the crisp white snow. Nights lasted longer than the clock said they did. Why was no one coming? Did anyone know there was a crash? Our car had veered off the icy road, turning over and over again until we came to a resting spot in the embankment. Two more cars clanked and clattered as they collided with each other, tumbling over the tremendous cliff below. The deafening sounds continued as a few more vehicles slammed into one another before they descended down the side of a massive slope. This area was so remote that very few vehicles traveled on the stretch of road leading up the north side of that mountain.

At this steep terrain, no cell phone service was available. Anyone that got stranded had to rely on a good Samaritan that happened to be passing through. Chances are that most of the people in the wreckage were mountain folks, perhaps one or two tourists. Problematic was the deep snow that kept coming, it took hours just to walk one mile. The survivors in our car plus three others from two cars that landed in the embankment all set off on foot in search. We knew that getting to the cliff side of the mountain was going to be difficult. We also knew that there were at least three vehicles that slid over the cliff and we had to find those cars. Rummaging through our compacted vehicles, we found survival items that we could bring. Grabbing a duffel bag, we filled it with what we scrounged up. Our group ended up with two flashlights, several water bottles, one blanket, a tarp, crackers, protein bars, fruit, couple pairs of gloves, two lighters, and a half filled first aid kid. Daylight was burning, we had to get moving.

All of us knew rescue vehicles would not come and couldn't come in a blizzard. Unless someone saw what happened, it did not get reported. To make matters worse, no one could see the wrecked cars from the road, so there was no urgency and no one looking. Our team all agreed that the cars plunged over the north side of the cliff so we headed there. Group decision was to walk for three hours at a time then rest for 30 minutes. Along the way we gathered anything viable to our survival. Someone reached into his pocket and found a Swiss army knife that he carried "just in case."

Daylight was diminishing and would be gone in four hours. We needed to move. The next problem was wet clothes, we figured when we stopped to make camp and get a fire going, we could sit close and get dried. Wading through knee deep snow was a task and it was using up our energy but we were keeping warm as long as we were moving. About an hour in, we came across a river that was parallel to the trail we were carving out in the snow. Now we had a source of drinking water and perhaps a fish lurking in there somewhere. Food would be scarce as we were in the dead of winter, so we had to conserve the little bit we had. We learned that one of the survivors of our group was a former Marine and completed three tours in the Middle East. He became our leader.

Marching on, we came upon a clearing next to the semi frozen river. We would have a clear spot for a fire and could be seen if a plane was low flying, chances of that, slim to none. There was an open view to see if any animals were approaching. Rapidly we worked to set up a lean to with branches and pine brush we found and we used the tarp to create a floor. The solitary blanket we had would stretch over all five of us if we sat close together. It was so damn cold though! Our leader instructed us to get loose branches, bark and wood for the long night ahead. One of the benefits of being at the base of a huge chain of mountains was all the trees surrounding us. The lean to was placed under the shelter of a huge pine facing the open so we could see everything. Beyond that we went looking for large rocks to make a circle around our fire. Also, we needed small rocks to heat up in the fire place in our lean to for warmth. The Marine taught us that. He was spot on. Once we had our fire going and let those get rocks hot, we used a huge stick to knock them out and pushed them into our lean to. They retained warmth for hours into the night. Hunkering down for the duration, we all feared what we would see the next day, if we in fact survived it.

During the night, there was noise and shuffling around us. Springing into action, the retired Marine grabbed the thick knotted tree branch that he had sharpened into a spear. I hoped whatever was out there wasn't bigger than that spear! The remaining four of us got up and heard a screech and a "woot-woot!" A rabbit had been nearby and had been unfortunate as she was the end of that spear. Hurrying up, I stirred up the embers, gathered some more wood and got a fire going. Quickly we had that rabbit skinned, bled out and gutted and on a massive stick for roasting. For tonight or this morning, we would not be hungry. Newly energized and rested, we decided we had better get a move on. Once we put out the fire and gathered our gear, we were off.

For today, the sun was shining as a guiding light force. The winds had died down but it was still hovering around zero degrees. As long as we kept moving we were okay. We were at the base of the cliff but we knew we still had a couple of miles ahead of us. Around noon, we decided to stop for a break and to eat the protein bars. As we sat hunched over, blowing on our hands for warmth we heard a woman's voice. "Search for me and I will help you find," she spoke. "What does that mean?" The five of us looked at one another trying to figure out where she came from. She had no shoes on, a long flowing sheer dress, fringed brown shawl wrapped around her and thick steel grey hair was flowing down her back. "What is your name m'am," I asked her. She never looked at me, it seemed as though she was looking through me. Saying it again, "search for me and I will help you find," she whispered. "Help us find what," the three of us chimed in. "You will find only what you seek, nothing more," she said speaking from years of wisdom. "But why should we search for you when you are standing before us?" one of the survivors asked. "Search for me and you will know," she said pointing to her chest. As quickly as she showed up she was gone, disappearing into the woods along the half-frozen river.

She woke me up with those words. My life was going along fairly smoothly, a few difficult setbacks happened and they were now in the past but in general things were good. Lately though, I had felt a void which gave me a longing for something. My feelings that I needed something more were very strong. Here we were out searching for survivors of a crash but she wanted us to search for her? Why? What was to be found? Whatever it was, I wanted to find it. Newly recharged, we set out to hopefully locate survivors. Daylight was burning and we needed to be blazing trails. In those moments I knew I was searching for more.

Challenging bitterly cold, seemingly never- ending depths of snow and frigid temps made me think we would never make it. We were tired, cold, hungry and felt defeated. I had to admit that there was a period that I felt defeated this year after my mate walked out on me with no explanation. During that time, I did feel like quitting and I lost a bit of my sparkle. Maybe that what I was seeking, I was trying to get my mojo back. Things in my business life were going fairly well but my need to do more was tugging at me. Not only was I searching in a snowstorm for survivors but I was also searching for answers in my own life.

Up ahead we saw something sparkling in the sunlight. It was hard to make out, but it was a large item. Our adrenaline kicked in and we began to sprint towards the object. As we ran to it, we saw that it was the entire front bumper of a car. Once we rounded the bend we saw more. There were pieces and parts of several automobiles scattered around the ground as if someone spilled out a jigsaw puzzle. Just then we all stopped dead in our tracks! As we looked we saw a van fully intact except for the hood and in it were people and waving at us. Relief and fear set in all at once. How would we be able to help them if we barely had enough stuff for ourselves? What would we do with the injured people?

As our group approached the van, we saw three deceased adults laying nearby in the snow. Knowing there was nothing more we could do for them, we pressed forward. Upon opening the door, we discovered a woman and her two young children, an elderly couple, a teenage girl and a man appearing to be around my age mid 40's. We also noticed blood, lots of it. The woman said she thought her arm was broken but her kids made it with no injuries. Elderly couple was shaken and the woman would soon need insulin, the man walked on a cane and said he was in decent condition. Teenager spoke up and said she had hurt her ribs but she could walk and function. As I looked at the man in his 40's, his eyes drew me in immediately. Instant connection was made. I had this feeling like I was home when I looked at him. He was sitting under a blanket and when he lifted it off him, it revealed that his leg was severely damaged down to the bone. He was hurt the worst of the group. Again, the woman appeared saying "seek me and you will find."

We had our work cut out for us as we assessed who we could help, who could go farther on for help and who would tend to the wounded. Our leader assembled two teams. One team was made up to go on and get help. The secondary team was caregivers. Team one was the former Marine, teenage girl, and two survivors that were part of our search group. I was in team two with the remaining occupants of the van and one more of our original group. Our leader determined that once they got back up to the road, it was approximately a five- mile walk to the nearest town and they would leave at daybreak the next morning. We were worried that they wouldn't make it, that none of us would make it. Survival mode was all that we had. A few of the team spent hours hunting whatever they could find and stock piled it for food. Snow was collected and melted down and put into water bottles for drinking. We all crowded into the van and slept for a few hours. None of us wanted to tell the other about our concerns and that we were stressing about this. There was not much hope as things were very bleak.

Somewhere along the way I had given up notions that hope could help things. I was a realist and things were what they were. Hope only created false illusions. Again, my thoughts turned to the woman. I couldn't wrap my brain around what she was saying. In the back of my mind, however I did know I was seeking something. I spent time with the passengers of the van patching them as best as I could and getting to know them. It was the man that I felt plugged into. Out here in this bone chilling cold, I felt warmth around him. I felt that I could see clearly now. I had the feeling that I had woken up from a dream, come out of the fog and walked into the most magnificent sunshine there ever was. Until this day, I did not realize that I had been seeking something.

As I got to know the man, I found out that he worked with homeless people. He owned a place called "Finding Home," where he helped misplaced folks get housing and assistance with getting their life in order. His facility provided resources necessary to help folks get a place of their own. Over the years he helped several hundred folks get off the streets. Ironically, I owned a business that rehabbed old houses for a living then sold them. I enjoyed my work, made a decent living at it but never felt completely fulfilled doing it. Suddenly I wanted to help his organization. I could find the homes and flip them and he could get folks placed into them. It would be a perfect fit. Alert now and senses heightened, I told him what I wanted to do. He said he needed a partner as his last one moved across country and if we survived this, we could talk.

During the next day we all shared our life stories and everyone pitched in to do what they could. As I wandered about looking for wood, I realized what the woman was saying. I had to seek hope to find my future. Hope was something I had stopped looking for. I just went about my days one after another. This man had given me hope again. Not only that, I was excited that I could be helping people and making a difference. Now I hoped that our rescuers would come and soon because the aged woman desperately needed insulin and the man's leg was in horrible shape. Hope was back in my heart to stay. All this time I had been searching but not fully seeing. My eyes are clear now and they are wide open.

Kimberly Cunningham has published two books: Undefined and Sprinkles On Top. Also published in: Evergreen Journal, NY Literary Mag Tears, Torrid Literature, NY Literary Mag Flames, From The Heart by International Poetry Press, Crossways Lit Mag, herstry.com, The Daily Abuse book, Blood Into Ink, Poetry Super Highway, Curtis Bausse, Silver Stork Mag, Diverseverse 3 and other works forthcoming.

This scriber holds a Bachelor's Degree in Education and Master's Degree in Curriculum and Instruction. Her blog is located at **undefined1blog. wordpress.com.**

You can find her short stories at:
https://www.amazon.com/-/e/B072WNW4XB?follow-button-ad-d=B072WNW4XB_author&captcha_verified=1&

Kimberly's two books can be found here:
http://www.lulu.com/spotlight/kimberlycunningham

The World of the Beasts

Yolanda Barton

Each Monday morning, Miss Thorne in her beige fuzz sweater
would make us stand and howl
with untrained, cracking voices, as she sponged the whippet spit
from her chewed gloves. I cannot recollect
her lined face, her practical boots
without thinking of her other, four-legged choir.

The Old Boys' Round Robin told me
that she had passed on peacefully
in her home. Did the pack sing
to its departed alpha, its chieftainess?
As in life, she was serenaded to the next world
by twenty-four voices aged below fourteen
mauling On Ilkley Moor Baht Aht.

I paused at the dining table,
with a waddling woodpigeon cooing its grief in the background.
Snowdrops were drooping their heads in the park,

and the rook, the minister, stalked through them down the aisle,
to caw the epitaph and stab with his beak
at the welcoming earth. Dearly beloved,
this woman, music teacher, whippet breeder,
wearer of hideous skirts like sacks, well-worn.
She is succeeded by Jupiter, Sable, Roger,
Claudius, Artemis, Aphrodite and Cassandra;
the good woman was of a rather pagan bent, loved the classics.
The rook's service ended, he took wing,
the white snowdrops shaking their shoulders.
His performance needed a Roman priest to tear a liver
from a cow, warm and portentous,
as a coda. Only the creatures gave meaning
to her life. We speak and sing in the language
of the world of beasts.

It's in the way the beasts dot our thinkers' writing,
the descendants of the cave-shaman
who read the flights of birds
and sent red rhinos and hyenas scaling stalactite walls:
this book is really about communists
and this, the exploitation of women
in a fascist police state. This hedgehog
with her slick slug in the wet road
is the poet's perception of your friend
who ignores the thug
lurking in that alleyway
in quiet complacency of the last drink, the last kebab.

Yolanda Barton is a poet, artist and author based in Oxfordshire, UK, though she grew up in Swindon in the nearby West Country. Yolanda has been writing since she was a young girl, achieving publication in children's anthologies, and sees poetry as a way to connect, convey ideas and preserve memory, including memories that are inconvenient to society or undesirable to authority. She also writes factual articles under a nom de plume for politics journals.

Yolanda has lived and worked in Nottingham, both during the boom years and the crash, and in South Korea and Taiwan, all of which strongly influences her work. In particular, her time spent volunteering in an orphanage in Korea – in which she moonlighted alongside her work in a state secondary school – shaped her view of the world. She has also studied at the University of Nottingham and Oxford, and was published at both universities, including in the Oxford Forum Journal, where she wrote about her insight into the rise of Taiwan's Sunflower Revolutionary movement.

More of Yolanda's work can be found in 'Further Into Darkness and Light' on Amazon; and the Blue Hour anthology at : https://thebluehourmagazine.wordpress.com/ or http://bluehourpressbookstore.bigcartel.com/the-blue-hour.

The Girls' Table
Joe Okonkwo

A spit wad just hit the back of my neck. Another one.

They been shooting them at me all morning. I told Mommy and Daddy 'bout how the boys be doing all kinda stuff to me—spit wads; tripping me; pushing me around in the bathroom. Daddy tell me to fight. He say better to get a bloody nose than be no sissy. But Mommy say I ain't got to fight, all I got to do is look them in the eye real serious so they know I mean business, and they'll stop.

I'm scared to fight them. But doing it Mommy way ain't easy either. But I guess Mommy way better than fighting.

Miss Carson still at the board, teaching math. She showing us *greater than* and *less than*. I like Miss Carson. She got long, black braids all the way down to her waist. She wear a headband that match her dress—a African fabric, orange and yellow and light blue. Pretty colors. Pretty like Miss Carson. She explaining something to Latoya. Latoya always axing lots a questions. Miss Carson spend more time answering Latoya questions than anybody else's in our whole second grade class.

Mommy say if looking them boys in the eye real serious don't work, I should tell Miss Carson. But I don't want to be no snitch. People be getting even with snitches.

Another spit wad. I been wiping them off my neck all morning.

My heart beating fast. I need to turn around, look them in the eye real serious like Mommy say. But before I can turn, I hear somebody whisper, "Pssst. Cedric."

Here my chance. I turn.

A spit wad smacks me right on my mouth.

Dean the one did it. He sit in the row next to mines, a few seats back. Dean wear a black doo rag. We ain't supposed to wear no doo rag in the classroom. Miss Carson always telling him to take it off. He don't, though. Dean don't never listen. He smiling all big and bright. Like bright could hide the meanness. It don't. He holding a white plastic knife from the lunch room. He been using it to flick the spit wads at me, putting them on the blade part, bending it back, letting go so the spit wad flies. Dean laughing out loud. Some of the other boys—his crew—they laughing, too.

"Is there something you gentlemen would like to share with the rest of us?" Miss Carson say. Nobody say nothing. Miss Carson shake her head. "Know what, guys? It's 1997. I'd think you'd act a little more civilized." She go back to explaining *greater than* and *less than*.

The spit wad stuck on my top lip. Like it's glued. I brush it off. I got to be careful not to lick my lip. I don't want to taste Dean nasty spit.

I turn back around and face the board.

"Pssst," Dean say. "Turn around again. Faggot."

When I turned before, I forgot to look him in the eye real serious. Ain't no use now. I stay facing front. I should be listening to Miss Carson, trying to see what she writing on the board. But I'm too busy crying and trying not to show it.

*****

Miss Carson sending us to the bathroom to wash our hands before lunch. She sending us in groups. It's my group turn, even though Dean group still in there.

I don't wanna go in there. I wait outside the bathroom door. I'll go in when Dean come out. But he taking forever. I hate it when his group go before mine, 'cause he always in there real long and I'm scared to go in when

Dean in there. Maybe I'll skip washing my hands. Just today. But my hands got paint on them from art class. Mommy wouldn't want me eating with paint on my hands. And I got spit on my hands from wiping all them spit wads off my neck.

I go in.

It stink. Someone in a stall doing number two. The sinks is rusty and brown. Some of the knobs on the faucets is missing. People done wrote names and curse words on the white walls and they got yellow stains. Some of them stains is wet. There's a puddle of pee on the floor. Dean laughing and messing around with some older boys from fourth and fifth grade. He still got the plastic knife, the one he been using to flick them spit wads at me. He jumping at people with it like he Wesley Snipes in a action movie, and showing it off like that plastic knife's gold.

"Nigga, stop acting a fool," a fourth-grade boy say.

"Yo, Dean. You acting like it's a switchblade, dog," a large fifth-grader say. "That thing ain't even sharp."

"Yeah, it is," Dean say, like a wise guy. "I'm gonna prove it."

Dean strutting around. He trynna to impress the older boys, trynna act big like them even though he small like me. Trynna act gangsta. The good thing is he don't notice me. I'm drying my hands and thinking how lucky I be. I'm thanking god that Dean don't see me.

Then he do.

"Hey!" he yell. "Cedric! You gonna sit at the girls' table again today?" He turns to the older boys. "Yo, this nigga sit with the girls every day!"

They laugh so loud, my ears rattle.

"Why you sit with the girls, yo?" the large fifth-grader say. He so large, he got breasts.

"He a faggot!" Dean say.

The large fifth-grader push me. I fall on the floor. The floor grimy. People be messy when they wash they hands and water spill from the sinks and mix with the grime and make the floor muddy and now it on my hands and I just washed them. Someone still in that stall doing number two. It stink so bad, I hold my breath.

"That true?" the large fifth-grader say. "You a faggot-ass?"

He tall. He wider than me. He got fat cheeks and two chins and a tummy like a big ball. I look up at him, like looking up at a mountain. He keep coming toward me. I scoot back. Now I'm close to the puddle of pee. I don't want that nasty pee on me. It get on me, my clothes be wet and stinking and Miss Carson won't let me in the classroom and everybody'll laugh and when I get home I'll have to tell Mommy and Daddy why I be stinking.

I got to get up.

I got to look him in the eye real serious, and he'll know not to mess with me. 'Cause I'm a good boy. And they shouldn't treat a good boy like this. If I look them in the eye real serious, they'll see I'm good. They'll stop this. Please, god, let them stop this.

I get up. But I don't look nobody in the eye. I run out.

I can hear them laughing from all the way down the hall.

*****

Latoya and Paris playing with they dolls at the lunch table. Latoya doll black. Paris doll white. Latoya looking at Paris white doll, all jealous. Latoya wish *she* had the white doll. She want to comb that soft blond hair, have blue glass eyes smiling up at her instead a brown ones.

I want to play with they dolls. I want to hold them, comb they hair, dress them, tuck them in at bedtime, lay they pretty heads on the pillow next to me. I want to ax Latoya and Paris to let me hold they dolls. But I know better. Bad enough I sit at the girls' table. If kids see me playing with dolls, too, they be laughing at me even worse. Latoya and Paris don't mind me sitting here, but the boys do. Even some of the girls be cutting they eyes at me, sucking they teeth. The boys sit behind us. Sometimes I hear them say *sissy*. Or *faggot*. Sometimes they whisper it. Sometimes they shout it. We can sit wherever we want in the lunch room, but the boys always hang together and the girls just want to be around each other. I don't sit with the boys 'cause I don't know how to talk 'bout ball and video games and rap. I don't like they nasty jokes 'bout girls' private parts and what grownups do in bed. I don't like how they always acting a fool and tripping people and flicking spit wads and calling people *nigga.*

Is something wrong with me?

Everybody think so. Daddy think so. He always ax, *Why you don't play ball? Why you don't stand up for yourself? Why you so skinny? Why you don't act like a boy supposed to act?*

I guess something *is* wrong with me. If everybody think so, if my own Daddy think so, then it must be.

"You want to trade dolls for one night?" Latoya say to Paris. Latoya looking at Paris blond doll like she want it so bad she could eat it up. Paris look at Latoya black doll and scrunch her face up. "Please, Paris? I'll be your best friend."

"Girl, you already my best friend," Paris say.

They trade dolls. Latoya all happy, but Paris frowning like she can't stand no doll the same color as her.

At least she got a doll.

I'm watching them, holding each other dolls, dreaming 'bout what it be like to hold one in my arms, pat the soft hair, look into the smiling face, thinking how a doll face look innocent and pretty. But I'm a boy. I should like football and basketball. But football and basketball ain't gentle. They ain't sweet. Dolls is. You can get hurt playing ball, but don't nobody get hurt playing with no doll. When you play ball and you make a mistake and the team lose, everybody be mad at you. They be yelling and cursing, talking 'bout how stupid you be for making them lose, for letting them down. But you can just take a doll to your room and play with it all quiet and don't nobody get hurt. Don't nobody feel let down.

I feel something on the back of my neck. It ain't no spit wad. Spit wads don't hurt. This hurt. Like somebody struck a match on my neck and then held it there and let it burn.

"Dean!" Latoya shout. "What you doing?"

I turn around. Dean standing right behind me, grinning. He holding the plastic knife. It got red on it.

"I told them it was sharp," Dean say, looking at the knife like he proud of it. Like he proud a hisself. He walk away, toward the table of fifth-grade boys. They all looking my way. Dean walking like a big man. That large fifth-grader who pushed me in the bathroom, he high-fives Dean.

I feel the blood dripping down my skin. Like a insect crawling down my neck. I know it's staining my collar, the back of my shirt. I wipe my neck. My hand red.

"We got to tell Miss Carson!" Latoya say.

"Girl, I ain't no snitch!" Paris say.

"Cedric's our friend. We ain't letting Dean get away cutting our friend. Come on!"

Latoya take me by the hand and run, pulling me along. Paris come too, but she take her time. We don't say nothing when we get to the teacher table. We just stand there for a minute and wait for them to act like they notice us. Miss Carson ax us what we need. She look different from the other teachers 'cause a her African clothes and her braids. The other teachers be looking at us all serious, like they don't like us interrupting they lunch. Latoya do all the talking.

"Let me see, Cedric," Miss Carson say.

Some of the teachers watching, shaking they heads. Some keep eating and don't pay us no mind.

Miss Carson been acting like she can't be bothered, but something change when she see my neck. She grab a napkin quick and tell me to hold it against the cut. "Press hard. Dean did this?" She been talking low and sleepy-like before, but now she loud. Her eyes all big.

"Yes, ma'am!" Latoya say.

"Yes, ma'am," Paris whisper. She looking at the floor.

I don't say nothing. I'm too shamed. All these teachers sitting here, knowing something wrong with me. I want to cry.

Miss Carson send me to the nurse. The nurse wipe the cut with some-thing that sting, then put a Band Aid on it. "Leave that on for a couple of days," she tell me. "Don't want that cut getting infected. Lord have mercy. I don't know why you kids treat each other the way you do."

She send me back to class. Miss Carson waiting for me outside the room. Dean with her.

"Well?" Miss Carson tell Dean. "Don't you have something to say to Cedric?" Dean don't say nothing. "You're not going to apologize?" Miss Carson sound mad. Look mad, too. Not mad like when the class be acting up and won't nobody be quiet. She a different kind of mad. She walking back and forth so fast, her braids is swinging. And her mouth all closed and tight. Like she so mad she might hit Dean. "You're already in trouble, young man. Don't think your parents won't be told 'bout this." She put her finger in Dean face. It's shaking. "Now you apologize right now."

Dean look at me like I gross him out. "Why shouldn't I cut him? He just a boy who sit with the girls."

Miss Carson send him to the principal office. I go in the classroom. It's noisy when I walk in, but it get quiet quick. Everybody looking at me. Latoya must a told them what happened. That girl got a big mouth. I sit at my desk. I know everybody behind me looking at my neck, the Band Aid on it. Miss Carson start teaching spelling. My favorite subject. But I can't concentrate. I keep thinking 'bout Mommy and Daddy and what they'll say when they see my neck and I have to tell them what happened. They'll be disappointed in me. *Why ain't you look him in the eye real serious?*, Mommy'll ax. And Daddy'll say, *Why you didn't fight back?*

I guess I'll tell them I ain't have no chance. I ain't see him coming.

Joe Okonkwo's debut novel *Jazz Moon*, set against the backdrop of the Harlem Renaissance and Jazz Age Paris, won the Publishing Triangle's Edmund White Award for debut fiction.

Road Gators
Carl Palmer

The four-foot strip of tractor trailer truck tire on the side of the road gets Addison talking. He points at the rubber traffic litter and starts telling of another adventure from his youth back in Hamlet, North Carolina. Just as with every story about his hometown, he begins by reminding me that the great saxophone player, John Coltrane, grew up in Hamlet, and Bandit, the original 1977 Pontiac Trans Am of the movie, *Smokey and the Bandit* sits on blocks by a double-wide just outside of town.

A.G., as he was called back then, and still today, along with three of his high school buddies, had all recently enrolled at the Richmond Community College to put off the draft a bit longer. They did most everything together and agreed if one got called up for the Army, they'd all go in together.

As usual, on a Saturday night, they were enjoying an evening of camaraderie and beer, not all that drunk, but not all that far from it. It was probably a combination of both not knowing when to stop drinking and not knowing how to safely pull off the road onto the shoulder which contributed to having the Player family sedan ending up in the ditch on its roof.

They were on the new stretch of Highway 177 coming back from the Community Center Go-Go party in Hoffman. All the boys knew the pretty girls lived there where girls loved to dance and rumored to do other things, too.

Laughing and all talking at once, A.G. pulled over to the side for a pit stop. Right away it was obvious that the soft shoulder was narrower than it looked and the slope was steeper than he expected. Since it was all just recently constructed, the ground was not yet solid under the freshly spread gravel and sod. As A.G. felt the car go down off the edge, he quickly turned the steering wheel back up towards the road.

As he did, the front wheels dug in, the car leaned downward in slow motion, tipped, rolled gently onto its passenger side and then stop on its top, upside down halfway to the bottom of the ditch. All this without a sound from the car or the boys inside.

It had gone in smoothly and the ground gave way to the weight without scraping or scarring the car's finish in the newly sown grass. They surveyed the situation, made a plan to just roll it down a little further so it would be back right side up on its wheels and then drive it on out, none the worse.

To aid the roll-over operation, the boys found some discarded sections of tire tread on the side of the road, a couple as long as four foot. These hunks of recap tire are commonly called gators in that part of the south. They looked like the partially submerged bodies of those alligators floating in the swamp down by Crawford Lake.

Each boy grabs a gator and each hollers out into the night. They'd failed to realize the rubber tires were reinforced with steel mesh belts that immediately dug into their arms and chests.

The plan worked. The car rolled down the rubber cushioned ramp to the bottom of the ditch without a single flaw on the body of the sedan. The only casualty was the radio aerial. Now broken, the only station the radio would pick up was WYFQ, a religious channel out of Wadesboro. It was his mom's favorite anyway, so it'd do until A.G. could get a replacement antenna.

The bodies of the boys, scratched and scarred, were the topic of all conversation. Every time the story was told it grew just a little bit better, soon becoming a Hamlet legend of those fearless four boys rasslin' rabid wild gators back into the swamp, making the community safe again.

All four left for Fort Bragg two months later, got matching tattoos right after basic training and ended up making the military their career as lifers in the United States Army.

A.G. always has time to tell a story, share a cold drink in the shade and, if you ask, may just show you his gator tattoo.

Yard Darts
Carl Palmer

Wendy tells us ahead of time Harold is king of his yearly yard dart tournament, warns me on how he embarrasses all comers with his backyard bravado.

Judy had mentioned I was a pretty good horseshoe player back in the day, so Wendy's hoping I may be the one to beat her boasting husband at his own game and invites us to their annual summer patio party.

The men gather by the tub filled with cold bottles of beer while the women set the patio covered tables with massive amounts of food.

As anticipated, after dinner and a couple hours of beer, Harold announces the tournament to begin. Each of us eight men is expected to play and, as in the past, throw a five dollar entry fee into the pot.

"Let's up the ante this year," Harold smiles, "ten bucks."

An underhand tossing method is used, same as when pitching horseshoes, however the 12 inch dart is much lighter than the regulation 2 pound 10 ounce horse shoe.

The distance is 35 feet between the two eighteen inch diameter plastic rings instead of the 40 feet between one inch round metal stakes measuring 15 inches out of the ground in horseshoes.

Harold's Scoring Rules:

Each player has two darts, either red or blue. Three points are earned for each dart landing inside the ring. One point earned for landing the closest outside the ring if the opponent is not in the ring. Tie throws cancel each other out.

Example: Red lands two in the ring for six points. Blue gets one in for three and one out for no points. Score: Three points for red. None for the blue.

The game goes to 21 unless one side gets to 11 before the other gets any points, which results in a Skunk.

Our eight names are put in the hat to determine who plays on each of the four two man teams the first round. Harold puts our names in blocks on his poster paper score board.

Rumor is he has a stack of sheets displayed in his garage from every year's past tournament game.

The four winners of the first round are then put in the hat for the next round of competition of two teams, leaving only one final winning team, Harold and me. We two are now set to go head to head for the final grand championship game.

Before we start, Harold asks loudly if I'd like to take a friendly side bet "just to make things more interesting."

The crowd cheers when I pull out a twenty and say, "But first, let's have another beer."

I drink my beer slow, throw a few practice shots back and forth while Harold plays the crowd.

Walking back, I mention that it's getting pretty dark and ask if he has a yard light.

Knowing the distance by heart and playing with home court advantage, Harold could easily throw with his eyes closed and hit the ring consistently.

"Oh, don't worry, it's not that dark. No more stalling. Let's get on with it. This shouldn't take long anyway," winking at the audience.

We flip a coin to see who throws first. Harold wins and quickly tosses his two darts, both stick slightly short of the ring. My two land dead center. Six to Zero.

Now my turn to throw first, both darts land in the ring. This time Harold's two darts go long.

A skunk. I win. Twelve to Zero.

The crowd goes wild. The king is dead.

Long live the king.

That next year when Harold breaks out the Yard Darts the two rings are tied together at the prescribed distance with a rope so they can't be "accidentally nudged" by someone's foot when it starts to gets a little dark.

Carl "Papa" Palmer of Old Mill Road in Ridgeway, VA now lives in University Place, WA. He is retired military, retired FAA, now just plain retired enjoying life as Papa to his grand descendants. Carl, Hospice volunteer, is a former Pushcart Prize and Micro Award nominee.

His works have been published in sixteen countries and in over 750 online and print journals to include *Voices in Wartime, Haiku Scotland, Lucidity, Form Quarterly, San Pedro River Review, Proud To Be, Antipodean, Centrum Press Anthology, Cadeus - Yale University, The Poetry Library - South Bank Centre, Post Road, Hudson View, Mobius, Trellis, Lummox, Clover, Columbia Review, Houston Literary Review, Floating Bridge, Anastomo, Kerovacs Dog, Kalyna Review, Sarasvati, Zocala Press, Voices Israel, Soliloquies, Poetry Super Highway, Ascent Aspirations, Calliope - Mensa, Poetry Atlas, Magnapoets, Dirty Chai, The Mom Egg, Punkin House Digest, Welter, Tipton, Dallas Review, Garbanzo, The Stony Thursday Book, Binnacle, Two Thirds North - University of Stockholm, Penwood Review, Penine Ink and Whispers in the Wind.*

To read and listen to more of Papa's prose and poetry Google "Carl Papa Palmer"

MOTTO: Long Weekends Forever

Blown Away

Thomas Healy

Suddenly the telephone rang in the kitchen but Barnaby didn't bother to answer it, figured it was just another solicitor eager to sell him something he didn't need. The only calls he received in the evening anymore seemed to be from sales people. Shaking his head, he looked again at the three snapshots of Amy spread across his desk. He took all of them from his kitchen window where he often stood and watched her play on her front lawn with other girls in the neighborhood. Two were of her washing the hull of a speedboat that belonged to one of her mother's many men friends, the other was of her awkwardly attempting a cartwheel. Though it was nearly impossible to make out her face, he decided to use the cartwheel picture because it caught the carefree spirit that he always associated with her.

On his old Crosley record player Bill Evans played "Sleeping Bee," and he smiled, remembering Halloween when Amy dressed up as a bumble bee with plastic milk straws serving as antennae.

On top of the cartwheel snapshot he set a transparent glass paperweight and, with a carpenter pencil, carefully traced around the base of the weight. Just as carefully, after removing the weight, he picked up a pair of scissors and trimmed a little inside the tracing mark so that the picture was slightly smaller than the base of the paperweight. Then he applied a thin layer of decoupage glue to the bottom and set the picture on the glue, pressing down firmly with both thumbs. It would take a while to dry but he was not in any hurry and just stared at the picture now enclosed in the paperweight, marveling once again at how enthusiastic Amy was, always willing to accept any challenge it seemed. She almost looked as if she were about to burst out of the enclosure.

After the picture dried, he got up from his desk and set the paperweight on a shelf above the file cabinet. There were two other weights on the shelf that also contained pictures of Amy he took from his kitchen window. He still found it hard to believe, thought initially there would only be the first one he made, which he intended to present to her when she returned home. Now he doubted if she would ever return.

*

Barnaby was nearly eleven when he got his first paperweight---a glow-in-the-dark oyster's pearl fashioned from hand blown glass. It was a gift from his Uncle Caleb who bought it in Okinawa when he was stationed there as a Marine. He had no idea what it was, though, and had to ask his uncle who laughed and told him.

"But I don't have any papers."

He laughed again. "Everyone has things they don't want to blow away. And this is what you use to keep them in place."

Throughout his enlistment, his uncle sent him paperweights from all the different places he was posted. They were dark and luminous, transparent and opaque, some half a foot tall and others as small as robin eggs. By the time he began high school he had close to a dozen and was eager to add more to his collection. Others his age spent the money they earned after school on candy and comic books but he used his to purchase paperweights.

His third year in college he desperately needed money to cover an emergency room bill and was compelled to sell his collection, which had grown to almost sixty pieces, and assumed his interest in paperweights was over. He was mistaken, though, and within a few years had collected nearly twice as many as he had before. What he thought was an adolescent hobby had become an obsession so it was difficult to resist the urge to add to his collection. The shelves in all the apartments he resided in were stacked with paperweights and even after he and his late wife moved into a house of their own the shelves there were soon filled. Still he continued to purchase more paperweights, few of which were very valuable, and stored them in the basement in boxes and crates and a couple of old steamer trunks.

Shortly after Amy and her mother moved into the neighborhood, they learned about his curious collection and one day approached him and asked to see it and he was more than happy to oblige and showed them the paperweights in his living room. Amy, in particular, was fascinated by the crystal pineapple weight on the mantel above the fireplace, staring at it for a couple of minutes while he discussed some of the other pieces in the room.

"You must've been collecting for quite some time," Mrs. Hester remarked at one point.

"Since I was about Amy's age, maybe a year or two older."

"I imagine your collection must be worth quite a lot of money."

He grinned. "Oh, some paperweights are worth thousands of dollars, especially those made in France in the middle of the 19th century, but those aren't the kind I can afford. Mine are knickknacks not treasures."

"They sure look valuable."

"Well, they are to me but I doubt if they would be to anyone else."

She nodded. "You don't see paperweights much anymore. Now that I think of it I don't believe we have one in the office where I work."

"Desks aren't cluttered with papers in this electronic age, I guess, so paperweights have pretty much become a thing of the past."

"They still sell them, though."

"They do but not like they use to."

"I'd like to have one," Amy suddenly declared, still standing in front of the pineapple weight.

He chuckled, tapping her on the back of the neck. "Well, I'm glad I'm not alone."

*

Not quite a week later, Amy knocked on his back door and asked if she could see some more pieces in his collection. She was alone but assured him her mother knew where she was so he invited her in and showed her the paperweights in his den. Again, she seemed fascinated by the decorative objects but even more she seemed to enjoy listening to him talk about them. Some of the weights came from halfway around the world and she almost felt transported to some of the exotic locales as he spoke.

The day after next, she returned to his house and he offered her a cup of hot chocolate and let her see some more pieces. Soon she was visiting him a couple of times a week, always right after she got home from school, and though she continued to be interested in his collection, she also enjoyed talking with the older man and seeking his advice about different concerns in her life.

"You know what?" she blurted out one afternoon, after he suggested some courses she might consider signing up for when she started high school in a few years.

"What's that, dear?"

"You know me better than anyone."

"How can that be?" he asked, startled by the remark. "I've only known you a couple of months."

"I don't know but you do, Mr. Barnaby."

Flattered, he suggested they make a paperweight together and, at once, her eyes became the size of poker chips as she followed him into the kitchen. From a cabinet he took out a small jar along with a penguin-shaped eraser that looked like a prize found inside a cracker jack box. Then, under his guidance, she glued the eraser to the bottom of the jar, poured in a quarter of a cup of corn syrup, and filled the jar with tap water. Next, she added a few drops of burnt orange food coloring, stirred the mixture with an ice cream stick, and added some sequins. Once the lid was glued back onto the jar, he cautioned her to let it dry for a couple of hours then, if she wished, she could shake the new paperweight and watch the sequins float like snowflakes.

*

Barnaby and his late wife didn't have any children, which was a mutual decision he later came to regret, so he began to think of Amy as the daughter he never had and looked forward to her visits in the afternoon. A bundle of vitality, she seemed unable to conceal whatever was on her mind, and the more she talked the more concerned he became about her and the issues she had with the different men in her mother's life. Repeatedly he urged her to start a collection of her own, hoping that might take her mind off her troubles for a while, and one afternoon, as an incentive, gave her the pineapple paperweight she so much admired.

"I can't accept this, Mr. Barnaby."

"Please, dear, I insist."

"Really?"

"Really."

"Oh, thank you, thank you," she stammered, after giving him a peck on the cheek. "This is, by far, the most beautiful thing anyone has ever given me."

The following afternoon, to his surprise, he received a visit not from Amy but from her mother whose eyes appeared a little narrower than usual as if she had just got out of bed.

"Hello, Mrs. Hester."

"Hello."

"What can I do for you today?"

Grimacing, she folded her arms across her chest. "Oh, I just wanted to thank you for the lovely paperweight you gave Amy yesterday."

"It was my pleasure."

"She couldn't be more pleased."

He smiled. "I'm glad."

"Amy is very fond of you, as you are aware I'm sure, but I don't think it's a good idea for her to come over here so often."

"Believe me, Mrs. Hester, she isn't bothering me. Not at all. Truth be told, I look forward to her visits."

"Well, you see, I don't think it looks right for her to be over here without me or some other adult."

His jaw tightened. "What are you implying?"

"I'm not implying anything."

"You damn well are."

"All I'm saying is that it doesn't look good for a young girl to be alone in someone's home who's old enough to be her grandfather for a couple of hours every other day."

"I really resent what you're suggesting, Mrs. Hester. I've never done a thing anyone would regard as improper. Not a blessed thing. And I'm shocked that you'd ever think that I had. All I've done is listen patiently to your daughter talk about all the problems she has to face living with you and all your men friends."

She glared at him for a long moment. "Amy will not be coming over here anymore, sir. And if you try to get in touch with her, I'll call the police."

"You bitch!"

"I may be that but I'm also her mother and I'm telling you to stay the hell away from her."

*

The wretched woman got her way because Amy never again set foot inside his house. And whenever he was out in his yard and saw her and waved, she ignored him and went back into her house. He assumed her mother had lied and told the child he was the one who didn't want her to visit him anymore. He considered writing her a letter to explain that was what her mother wanted, not him, but was afraid the hideous woman would find out and make good on her threat and report him to the police. So he decided not to and resigned himself to looking at the girl from his kitchen window. Some day he hoped she would learn the truth but suspected it might not be for quite some time.

Not quite two months after Amy's last visit, flyers appeared in the neighborhood with the word "MISSING" printed above her picture. He was surprised, to be sure, but not entirely because he figured she could not remain in that house much longer. He always suspected she really came over to talk with him in order to get out of her house for a while. Along with others in the neighborhood he passed out flyers and looked for signs of her along the riverbank and in some on the parks in the area. He even reconciled with her mother, to a degree, who had no idea where her daughter was and who, if anyone, might have taken her and was beside herself with grief. He doubted if Amy would ever return, even though that was why he made a paperweight every year to give to her when she did, but deep down he knew that was very unlikely to happen. Really he made the paperweights so he wouldn't forget her. These days it was so easy to forget people, their faces and voices slipped away almost as quickly as their names.

Thomas Healy was born and raised in the Pacific Northwest and recently published a novel, "Red Weather," as a web book by Tri-Screen Connection.

The Goodwoman
Kirsty A. Niven

I had lived in that tiny fishing village on the west coast of Scotland my whole life, Aultbea. Most parts of that life are fading now, I'm forgetting too much. I just remember the main events, the parts that brought me here. I'd been married to someone, a man named John, pushed into it by my parents just as every woman was back then. He was not a cruel man, not under ordinary circumstances, but equally he never cared for me. Yet I convinced myself that I could have done worse, or so I believed at the time.

One day, as I was taking my daily walk along the shoreline, gathering dried seaweed for the fire, I met someone. I toppled over whilst trying to avoid standing on a heap of jellyfish on the cobbles, and a man caught my arm. Only a moment before, there hadn't been a person in sight. For a split second, in my pious naivety, I almost believed him to be an angel. He towered above me by at least a foot – by far the tallest man I'd ever encountered. His chalky skin glowed ethereally, fluorescently bright on that humid but cloudy day, and his blue eyes startled me with their ghostly, animalistic gaze. I should have known then that he wasn't ordinary. I should have predicted the impact that he would have on my small, domestic life.

The man's name was far too ordinary to rightly belong to him –Alistair. His voice was deep and had a velvety quality to it, but he rarely spoke. Words were never necessary with us. I fell in love with him immediately; the minute the question "Are you okay?" tumbled from his lips. I never understood what he saw in me but I chose to live in the moment without questioning his motives. I was too happy to allow myself to ruin a perfect thing by worrying. I became reckless, failing to care whether my stubby little husband discovered our affair. I know for certain now that that selfish little man would have murdered him outright – well, he would have if it were within his abilities.

Our affair went on for six blissful years, yet John remained unaware. I passed off three of Alistair's children as his – all beautiful little boys – but he was too stupid to see the truth. It was that June when Alistair disappeared. He was supposed to meet me at the end of the thin, crumbling path that led from my garden to the cobbled beach. I waited there, leaning on the old oak tree that stood there. I waited for a couple of hours, maybe more. He'd said that he would be there at midday, as usual, but he didn't appear. I returned to that spot again and again, just in case I'd made a mistake. He was never there. Sometimes, as I walked towards that spot, I'd think he was there, leaning against that tree with his dark curls flying around in the wind. It was after this that I had a revelation. I realised that despite the time we'd spent together, I had never discovered where he lived. Oddly, all that I knew was that he lived beside the sea. Somehow this had never occurred to me, blissfully bewitched as I was. He had always been so secretive, so silent. A few times I even walked up and down the coast as far as I could, but I didn't find any sign of him. Several months passed and reluctantly, I gave up.

As our sons grew up, they became increasingly and blatantly different but it was impossible to pinpoint. They were unlike all other boys of their age. Their smiles had the same mysterious luminescent edge to them that their father's had, but their movements were awkward and jerking. They often seemed like fish out of water, particularly worrying once I realised that each one of them was a strong swimmer. In fact, they all spent the majority of their days, even the most bitterly cold, swimming in the sea. That was why I had carved out that little path that led directly to the beach, crossing the little patch of woods in between our garden and the beach. Just like their father, the children had no real aptitude for words.

It was around about then that I could tell that my husband was becoming increasingly suspicious. It was inevitable really – the children I had let him believe were his were clearly too beautiful to truly be the product of our marriage. Their jet black hair and stormy eyes could not have come from him, with his balding sandy head and beady, yellow eyes. But he had never uttered a single word outwardly of it.

Then one sweltering hot summer day, two years after Alistair's disappearance, it all blew up. It was exactly the kind of day I would have longed to spend with Alistair, frolicking in the cool sea. I was sitting on the rusty old bench that sat at the back of the garden, sheltered by the overgrown branches of the rowan tree. I'd just gotten back from collecting seaweed and had placed it with the fallen branches in the corner of the garden to dry. The boys were chasing each other in clumsy circles. Glass shattered from within the house. I quickly hushed the boys and I ran as quietly as I could towards the house. Just as I reached the half open back door, it swung at me violently and John burst out in a blind, screaming rage.

He had clearly been set off by the gossip that was beginning to travel around the village of my infidelity. I would never deny my actions; it was inevitable that the truth should emerge someday. I could never have been made to feel ashamed of something which had inspired so much happiness. I didn't once even attempt to lie whilst he bellowed at me, although I barely listened to his ranting. I knew for certain that his anger did not spring from any jealousy or love he felt for me, despite our decade together. His rage derived from shame at having been fooled by a woman, at having wasted money and time pretending to care for another man's children. Once he'd finished with his petty tantrum, he stomped into the house and resurfaced within a few minutes dragging a suitcase behind him. He vanished from the village without a word to anyone, leaving me to fend for myself and the boys alone.

We somehow barely managed on our own, a high achievement in such a judgmental small village, but it was only due to the charity of an unknown benefactor. On the thirteenth day of every month, a basket would appear, sitting on the seat of the swing hanging from the enormous rowan tree in the garden. The basket always carried the comforting, salty smell of the sea and enough money for us to get by. Under normal circumstances, I would never have trusted such an unusual transaction but I had no other means of monetary gain. I was desperate to keep my family afloat. In order to excuse John's absence, I told everyone in the village that he was working away for a while and sending money back to us.

For two years this went on and my sons reached the ages of eleven, eight and six. My boys became gradually stranger yet, simultaneously, their surreal beauty continued to grow. Still, they spoke very little and only when necessary and their clumsy sense of balance worsened dramatically. Their skin began to toughen to a leathery texture. Once, Alexander, the eldest, had a strange patch of silky fur appear on his back and the youngest, Ross's fingers fused together into webbed flippers. I hid them all away, fearing any trouble that may have risen if the villagers noticed my children's abnormalities.

It was during this period of hibernation that John returned. The children were in bed and I was sitting at the kitchen table reading. I heard loud thumping at the front door and I jumped up to find out what was going on. I ran towards the kitchen door and peered round, seeing his silhouette through the opaque glass of the door. Suddenly he became completely still. He stayed like this for about a minute before the silhouette moved away. I let out a sigh of relief. Then, something smacked against the glass and slid down, leaving a trail of blood behind it. I heard his raucous laugh. He was blatantly drunk, although he had never touched a drop of alcohol throughout our marriage. I heard his clumping footsteps move away and then a low chortle. His dark shape swooped behind the glass and something rammed against the door. It rammed again. And again. The glass gave way and glass flew out everywhere, I ducked to avoid the worst of it.

When I looked up again, he was standing an inch away from me, staring with his bloodshot eyes. I could see the dead rabbit he'd thrown at the door lying awkwardly on the front step. Still glaring at me, he reached for the shelf to his left, picked up a plate and dropped it at my feet. Next he went for a wine glass. I watched on as he slammed it against the wall, lacerating his hand. He slapped me across the face, leaving his blood on my cheek, overwhelming me with the strong reek of whisky. He pushed past me roughly and went for the stairs, stomping up them and leaving clumps of mud behind him, flaking off of his falling apart boots. I followed him warily, quickly picking up some of the broken glass while he wasn't looking. He burst into the boys' bedroom, shouting that he knew what they were. In a strange way I wished he had told me then, I longed for enlightenment. He bellowed that the boys were abominations. He lunged for the first bed and pulled Alexander out of it, throwing him towards the corner. I tried to stop him from doing the same to Sam but he sent me flying across to the other side of the room. By the time I looked up again, he had cornered all four of us. He pushed the wardrobe towards me, blocking me off from him and the boys, with only a narrow block of visibility. I could only see my boys, standing in a row, just as he had told them to. I shoved and shoved against the barricade but I could not break through.

Alexander, Sam and Ross stood perfectly still, obedient and blank-faced as he paced before them, examining their milky white faces scrupulously, still dragging me with him. I heard the faint rustling sound of his hand rummaging within his pocket. He approached Sam first, crouching down to meet his height. John placed his hand on Sam's shoulder, and looked him in the eye. Then I heard Sam gasp as John moved his hand towards his cheek. John lowered his hand, letting me see that he was pressing a knife against my son's face. I threw myself against the wardrobe again, but the wood refused to give way. John laughed malevolently. He slowly caressed Sam's cheek with the knife before turning to grin at me. The boys continued to stand there, ignoring my pleas with them to run. John pivoted, now focussing his attentions on Alexander. He didn't have to crouch to look him in the face; Alexander was tall for his age. John bared his teeth in a monstrous grin as he plunged the knife into Alexander's stomach. The blood spread out like a drop of ink on blotting paper across his body, as he fell softly to the ground, dead. His face remained angelic despite the grotesque volume of blood spilling out all over the floor.

I screeched at Sam and Ross to try to escape. Sam looked at me blankly, strangely deaf to my pleas and Ross tried to pull him away as he began his escape, realising now the danger he was in. Sam wouldn't budge; he simply stood at his fallen brother's feet, staring on silently with tears streaking his ashen face. As Sam stood staring, John lunged towards him and stabbed him in the back. Sam's eyes hardened, bulging coldly from his face – still transfixed with his brother's corpse. He fell to his knees and curled into a ball before suddenly becoming limp. Still struggling with the wardrobe, I reminded Ross he must move. The wood was beginning to give way just as Ross fled from the room, John tearing after them. I smashed through the back of the wardrobe with my elbow, finally and burst through it, following them, grabbing a chunk of the splintered wood for a make-do weapon. As I tore around the corner, John had trapped Ross against the wall. I ran at him and dug the wood into his shoulder blade, but when I pulled away, I saw that my attack had done no good. John had let go. My little boy slumped to the ground, his pale face serene with a violet hue. His neck was imprinted with finger print shaped bruises. One of them looked strangely like a miniscule broken heart.

I turned in blank horror to stare at John as he stepped back. Suddenly, he seemed disbelieving of his own actions. He had murdered my children for a crime I had committed, events that they had had no control over. John didn't really care whether they were 'abominations' or not. He was never religious. For a moment he stood there, glee and terror dancing and interchanging in his hawk like eyes, before marching out of the house, like a self-righteous soldier. His manner then was how I'd always imagined the faces of those who burnt women at the stake, accusing them of witchcraft – a look desperately insane in its beliefs.

I returned my attentions to the corpse of my youngest boy. He had only been six and unlike his brothers, he had always been tiny in comparison to other boys his age. I reached for his flipper like hands and clutched them, feeling as they cooled, as they solidified. I looked up to his little face, which resembled his father so much more than his brothers. I pushed his dark curls back from his face, examining its peaceful expression and closing his aqua eyes.

I remember nothing of what happened next. I only recall the repetitive, empty days and months that followed. They were buried at the end of the sprawling garden and a rowan tree was planted on top of each of their graves. Every night I would sit cross-legged before them, staring on in my static grief before smoothing a blanket over each grave. I continued to tuck my little darlings in for the night, even singing to them as I always had.

One night while I was doing this, John returned once more. He seemed to have been consumed by guilt, as he looked on with hollow eyes at my ritual of sorrow. The knowledge of his remorse did not comfort me. It did not comfort me at all. As he watched on, I stalked over to the rickety wooden shed that was once his. I retrieved his rusty wood axe. I walked calmly towards him. He remained wordless as I stood before him, axe in hand, glaring at him venomously. I lifted the axe, without hesitation, and swung it solidly through his fat neck. His balding head fell to the ground with a glorious thump. The expression on his face as the axe swung towards him had been shocked, and it had retained that look. John's head did not look like it had felt betrayed. I think he had come to me knowing the fate that he would encounter. He hadn't even recoiled; he knew he deserved to die.

I put the head in the wooden box he had stored his pumpkin seeds in and dragged his bloated body down the path that led directly to the sea. I heaved him in to the sea and watched on, wearing only my bloody, soaked nightgown, as he floated away. All of a sudden, I noticed a seal lounging nearby on the rocks. Its strange human like gaze was focussed on me; its expression was almost triumphant. It felt bizarrely comforting to assure myself that this creature understood me, did not blame me for my actions. It too, believed I was right. I had shaken the thought from my head, how could the seal even understand? I was trying too hard to persuade myself that I was not as evil as John. But ultimately I was. The seal began swimming towards me – still watching me, examining me.

The sinking feeling which had hovered nearby for so long finally overwhelmed me. Without a single thought, I dashed back to the house for the wooden box containing John's head and left it on the bay. I placed my grandmother's locket on top of it. There were three raven dark ringlets of hair inside of it. I sat myself down on the cool pebbles and squeezed my eyes shut tightly, still able to hear the sloshing sounds of the seal's approach.

There is nothing else left to do. I can sense a strange presence to my left now. The air surrounding it seems to quiver with excitement. I do not dare open my eyes. I failed our children. His cool leathery fingers rest on the crook of my elbow. He leans in to kiss my cheek softly. I whisper his name hoarsely. I stand up and walk into the sea. I won't allow myself a single glance backwards. The selkie follows me.

Kirsty A. Niven is from Dundee, Scotland where she lives with her husband and three cats. She graduated from the University of Dundee in 2013 with a first class degree in English. Her writing has appeared in a number of anthologies such as A Prince Tribute, Landfall and Betrayal: A Collection of Poetry and Prose on Betrayal and Being Betrayed. She has also had poetry appear in numerous journals and magazines, including The Dawntreader, Cicada Magazine, The Machinery and Dundee Writes. Kirsty's work can also be read online on websites such as Cultured Vultures, The Scottish Book Trust, Silver Birch Press and several others. She divides her writing time between poetry, her novel and a graphic novel.

You can visit her website - https://wutheringmites.wordpress.com/

THE MURMUR'S MACHINE
By Jeffrey G. Roberts

Once upon a time, in a distant and dark world, so irrelevant, dull and insignificant – indeed, a world so devoid of astronomical interest whatsoever that space-farers often slammed right into it due to terminal boredom just staring at it – there lived an equally brooding race of beings called Murmurs. Their world was the planet Murm. This fact was probably the only thing that did make sense on this moody ball of mud.

Now, in the galaxy where Murm comfortably resided, orbiting its equally boring sun, some seventy-five skedillion light years away there existed thousands of other civilizations, to be sure; most also supremely dull and unworthy of exploration. And each had their own particular set of complex and convoluted spiritual beliefs. Some involved the worshipping of lightning (which rarely ended well), while others adhered to the practice of inhaling the sweat of thousand-pound beasts called Poogs, believing this to be the ideal mystical way of opening a portal to the higher realms. But far be it for me to disparage the religious beliefs of other beings. But in the case of Murm, I shall make an exception – for theirs was truly idiotic.

Millennia earlier, several wise men – Meniscus the Broken, Loquacious the Incessant, and Flippus the Semi-virtuous, (and I use the term *wise* advisedly) – suddenly had an epiphany. It dawned on them that the reason their god was apparently not answering the prayers and supplications of the Murmurs, was that raising your voice and shouting was now considered to be an act of haughtiness; a show of arrogance. They reasoned that putting oneself on an equal standing with god by raising your voice to him, was blasphemy. And since no one on Murm wanted the moniker of blasphemer hanging over their heads, a codex, or holy book, was compiled to codify the principles of right living, known as *The Silent Epistles of Saint Ergelgerps the Numb.*

But how in the world could they have come to such bizarre conclusions? Well, call it a quasi-divine immortal legend (whether real or imagined no one ever really knew for certain) whose origins were lost in the mists of time. The most popular interpretation: eons ago, an ancient Murmur – whose name is lost to the ages, but most usually refer to him as Gootsneek – was hunting Poog beasts, hoping to kill one for dinner. But on his trek, he noticed a strange glow coming from a nearby cave. Upon entering it, and not realizing its entrance was a tad lower than his height, he cracked his head on the rock overhang. But seeing the source of the glow and staggering towards it, he had a revelation nevertheless. (True, the glow was coming from a simple bio-luminescent boulder, but through his bloody forehead and mental fog, he heard the *voice*!) And through said revelation was born the *Silent Epistles of Saint Ergelgerps the Numb,* and its admonition for global silence. And every Murmur from that day on who entered the sacred cave, solemnly attested to his holy edicts. (Forgetting for the moment that everyone who entered the sacred cave cracked their head on the identical spot, receiving the identical vision. Exceptional intellect was not high on the evolutionary menu back then). And down through the centuries, it was faithfully written down, and codified. Thus the legend was born. The rest is history – or lunacy, depending upon your point of view.

And from that day to this, the Murmurs on Murm adhered to its strict code of almost silent communication – until it involved *all* facets of life on their world. And of course, it soon became apparent that this was a very bad idea indeed. But no one *dared* question the holy writ. It would have branded them a heretic *and* a blasphemer – not to mention being blasted into zoo dust by an angry creator.

To be sure, some doubted the teachings of *Saint Ergelgerps the Numb*, but few were brave enough to speak up. It was never conclusively proven, (nor did anyone possess the testicular fortitude to try) but this fearful attitude might have had something to do with the incident their holy books referred to – in hushed tones – as The Great Mocking. Murm history records that 2,888 years ago, one Nunk Bavoon, a disenchanted grape stomper and Poog herder, thoroughly disgusted at having to ask "What?" in hushed tones, 9,347 times a month, and thoroughly inebriated, staggered into the street one day, raised his fist heavenward, and screamed "You stink!" Whereupon a boulder the size of a buffalo fell from the sky, promptly flattening him.

No one ever uttered a word louder than a whisper after that. True, in the centuries to come it was determined that Mount Boukva had a minor eruption on that very date and time. Also true was poor Nunk Bavoon's extreme bad luck to be standing precisely in the path of its volcanic excretions.

"But one thing had nothing to do with another," wise men of old eventually pronounced. "We understand now how volcanoes work. But the blasphemous Bavoon was squished by God for his arrogance – plain and simple. One was geological, and one was divine providence."

And that was the end of it. They would have sacrificed a virgin to appease and silence the insolent volcano – but they couldn't find any. Besides, the spiritual damage was done. (It didn't help that one of Murm's moons, actually just a giant asteroid, had the shape of an accusatory finger. And guess who it was perpetually pointing at?)

For as long as anyone could remember, homes, offices and government buildings – indeed, every construction project on Murm had, within easy reach, a large bucket of water placed every few yards. Why? Simple: if a construction worker committed the unpardonable sin of say, striking his finger with a hammer, with the resultant overpowering urge to scream obscenities in several colorful languages, the buckets were there to plunge his head into. In this way said screams would be effectively muffled. Better this, than incurring the wrath of an angry god. Amazing though, how many Murmurs died from accidental drowning. Indeed, many buildings often fell apart due to mumbled worker instructions being unintelligible. But if they *did* fall on people, they wouldn't dare cry out, due to - well – you know.

Fudamentalist Murmurs took their beliefs to ridiculous lengths, such as wearing specially designed flatulence suppressors, and voice mufflers. Singing was also reduced to mere whispering, making the preference of entertainer a poor vocation choice, to be sure. Night clubs were almost as dilapidated and empty as Murm churches. On Murm, arguments were largely non-existent. Unfortunately, ulcers – weren't.

But what the Murmurs never realized; the simple truth which never dawned on them: it wasn't that their prayers weren't being answered because they were raising their voices to God. They weren't being answered – because their god couldn't hear them! Indeed, the many times adherents of *The Silent Epistles of Saint Ergelgerps the Numb* beseeched their god with prayers – all *he* heard was a faint buzzing sound, and shooed them away, thinking them mere pesky mosquitoes!

And thus there came a time when Murm was on the verge of moral and spiritual collapse. Until one man – a Murmur, who marched to the beat of a different (albeit *quiet*) drummer, came upon the scene. An iconoclast who was determined to reawaken the glory – if you wish to call it that – that was once Murm. His name: Ning Broomglide.

"I love my world – but they're dimwits. I love my family – but they're idiots. I must prove *The Silent Epistles of Saint Ergelgerps the Numb* to be a tub of Poog crap. But how?" And he thought and pondered, ruminated and wondered – until it came to him like an epiphany one day while sitting under a fruit tree. And an apple fell on his head. "Ah ha!" he proclaimed. "I've discovered – the concussion!" And when he'd recovered, the *real* epiphany came to him. "I could shout heavenward at the top of my lungs. And I know God would surely hear me – the first Murmur to be heard by him in millennia. But I have no doubt that soon thereafter I'd either be locked up in a nut house, imprisoned, or worse – executed! Either way, I'd be forever branded a heretic and blasphemer, for committing the sacrilege of raising my voice to God. Then would come a dark age for Murm, and I'd never be able to prove that we've been wrong for three thousand years!"

It was truly a dilemma: how to shout without shouting – and not get caught doing it? It was here that he had his 2nd eureka moment: (not to have it under an apple tree). But it now dawned on him exactly how he was going to achieve his dream!

"I'll build a machine in secret, out in the forest; a grand machine pointed straight at heaven; a vocal magnifier. My whispered words to God will be amplified a million times! And when he finally hears us, a new Golden Age for Murm will emerge!"

Which is precisely what Ning Broomglide proceeded to do. And Rube Goldberg would have been proud. It looked like a calliope on steroids, and took him several months to build in secret. It had pistons and pumps – and what in the world was that smell? Like a combination of shellac, hot fudge, and kitten vomit. A giant curved trumpet-like megaphone made of glistening copper towered some twenty feet above the forest floor. And it in turn was connected to a tiny microphone, (considered satanic by Murm religion). Dials and switches, wires and gears, were everywhere. What were they all for?

And in the dead of night one fateful eve, while Poog beasts defecated with wild abandon, Murmurs planet-wide were accidentally drowning in water buckets, and flatulence was kept secret from angels on high, Ning Broomglide, hoped-for savior of Murm, snuck into the woods undetected, uncovered his machine – and turned it on!

And under the twin full moons of Murm, while they cast haunted shadows onto swaying trees, dozens of gears began turning, pumps started pumping, pistons began – well – pisting, and blue and green smoke began puffing out of a myriad of brass pipes. The giant curved horn began to vibrate, imperceptibly at first. Within ten minutes Ning was bathed in an eerie green light. This was his signal. He pulled a little chair up to the microphone, took a deep breath – but first put his hand over it and whispered,

"That's one small phrase from a Murmur; one giant shout for Murm-kind." *Hmmm, catchy*, he thought. Then he moved his hand away, took another deep breath, and said in a normal tone, "Hello God."

And a million squirtillion gazillion light years and 837 dimensions away, God himself – the Grand Creator, a.k.a. The Big Cheese, The I Am Because I Say I Am, The Big Kahuna, etc., was in a cosmic slumber in the Horse Head Nebula; with visions of how great it was that he invented sugar plums, to dance in people's heads. When all of a sudden a sound – like every creature in the universe farting & screaming simultaneously, rent all of creation with a force that sent every planet in existence to quivering and jiggling like lime Jell-o. It sent God reeling from his slumber, as he sat bolt upright.

"WHAT THE HELL WAS THAT!!??" he shouted. And he looked up, down, and across all of creation, to find the offending civilization that dared interrupt his siesta. "It figures! Murm! Those morons! They say I'm a vengeful God? Damn straight! Watch this!" And in an instant he took away all the Murmurs voice boxes! But, not being 100% heartless, he left them with a unique way to still communicate: telepathy. But in time – irony of ironies – a most curious thing began to occur: in their silence, the Murmurs finally rejected the idiotic teachings of *Saint Ergelgerps the Numb* – and turned inward with their now quiet minds – to music. Folk songs, actually. And though they could not sing, they could hear and play instruments of an incredible variety. And in time, folk tunes echoed across Murm. Loudly.

God thought he would lose his mind! Could these idiot Murmurs not be silenced? He seriously considered turning Murm into cookie crumbs. But not today. Not now. The irony was too humorous to stay angry.

And the moral of the story? Be careful what you wish for; the sounds of silence – may not be!

THE END

Jeffrey G. Roberts was born in New York City, raised in New York, and then South Florida. He attended Northern Arizona University, in Flagstaff, AZ, where he received a Bachelors degree in Writing, and a Masters degree in History. He currently resides in Tucson, Arizona, home of breathtaking vistas, and brain-boiling summers.

Orphaned Love

Subhadip Majumdar

She came to me like an orphaned shadow
Uprooted naked free
And embraced me
When I was floating
In my own world
Of deformed contours.

She claimed nothing
In that night of rain she warmed my bed
Later, as we lie down like two sailed away boats
I saw her half open lips trying to say something
Something, that would change us forever
But when I wake up in morning
I found an empty bed
And I saw in the mirror
My own face
Of orphaned love.

The Time to Go

Subhadip Majumdar

It is strange to feel that the sea has not changed after all when I am back here now.

Even after so many days, so much time, and the fading of perhaps twenty calendars, the sea remains the same. It always does...I think. It is obsessed in her own madness. She cannot stop or else she will die. But the moment the waves touched and splashed my face I felt like I had been kissed again.

The peace of returning to my home came to me and I remembered how I often took a train in this part of India and came here in my college days. No one knew about this beach back then. Well, except some backpackers, like us. The Russians, the French, and the Americans. One day I met one man on a train who told me about this little gem of Heaven. A place where the sea is untouched, and there is a calmness that is almost primitive. With that, and a little Keralite bag, the man was off!

That was the summer vacation I, with hardly any money, boarded the train with a second class compartment ticket. I still remember the feeling. The feeling of being somewhere where something changed in me. The sea gripped me, the world opened before me, and I became of the world. I started writing there on the beach and I felt like I had never written so clean, so pure, in times past. As if in the first sunrise, when I first saw the sea, I found the Meaning of Life and I knew what I had to do in order to acquire the things I desire out of my life. The sea that day made a man of me.

I walked through the grand boulevard of the beach city which overlook the sea. That old virgin beach has changed a lot, but not the sea. It is good to see that this remote, mapless place has earned such a reputation! So many hotels and hostels popping up everywhere. At the same time, I felt a strange pang of pain for those romances of sleeping on the beach with almost nothing around except the beauty and the wildness of a less traversed place. Footprints, there were hardly any footprints at that time on the sands. It was almost my own place of exile where I could take refuge at anytime I wanted. Life bleeds us so much that often you need shelter somewhere in a serene place. A place where you can cry out loud with no one to hear but your heart gets clean and empty and then you can breathe light. I still know these places around the laterite cliffs where there is still enough solace.

Day by day, solitude became my best surrender. I was walking towards that place when someone called me to stop. I turned back, and saw among the endless dark sea (aside from trollers blinking) that there was a lady, a Keralite woman, who stood smiling at me. A wind came from the sea and I somehow felt, 'this is a wind that wants to say something else'. She asked me to follow her. I did so by walking through a lovely colourful alley of souvenir and beach shops. Tourists, mainly Europeans, are here in large numbers. Some saluted me in French, and, I too replied, "Bonjour!", to them. There were some Spanish girls trying on jewellery, and among them, a boatman. A dark skinned, white moustached person walking back at days end with his net and tired face. The moon is shining now on the sea, and a girl is playing a tabla in a nearby instrument shop just beside a tattoo parlour. Again came the roar of the sea and the flight of the night bird.

At that time, a man came out from a small room full of shells and a painting of a Mohini Natyam dance and I heard him saying, "I can see that time has gifted you the pain of emptiness for being creative. You write, right?"

That moment broke something in me. Broke something, as well as collected. It is like in a strange paradox you are seeing your past life. The present moment hangs on to me with all the unwanted exposure of right and wrong and, 'what have I done to and with my life?'. I felt vulnerable. Why, I don't know. But at the same time, in me, a truth came to witness someone who has turned my life once. In a crowded train, on a warm sunny morning, forever.

"You are the man who first told me of this beach years ago.", I said.

He brought a stool, and we sat there. The roar of the surfs filled up the air in between us. He, with the yellow bulb on above his face, and the sound of the tabla still sounding from the instrument shop, smiled at me.

"Perhaps I was wrong to tell you about this beach. It destroyed you for being a normal man, didn't it?"

"I don't think so. I think that whatever has happened with my life, I would take it as a gift, and I am happy for that. We change all the time, in every moment. One new wave comes in and the old one goes out."

"Very well said. I am contented to see that you have identified your life in your own way. Yes, everything in every moment is breaking down. So much so, that even the old traces are removed in a whisper. Somewhere the remnants are there, so I am back at this beach, that which perhaps I discovered one night. The night I thought I would finish myself off. But this sea, this old, beautiful, seductive woman, wouldn't let me die that day."

"Why did you want to die? Besides, I forgot your name."

"I never told you. I hate to tell my name. It is the soul which has our real name. You can call me Altamiro. I am from Spain, but not from Altamira, a rhythm my name pronounces! In my thirties, I left Spain to travel the world, and after travelling Europe, came to Vietnam. There, among a desolated war country with nothing to see except beauty, I found Nadira. The woman with whom I fell in love. She was a courageous lady coming from a family of army men who fought the Vietnam war. Nadira and I lived together for ten years. As obsessive a couple may have lived, loving each moment we spent with each other. Then I got a good job of a travel guide in Syria. I, with all my knowledge of travelling the world, started working well and we were planning to get married and have a child. Nadira was not well for some days so we consulted a doctor. Even so, she still was not doing well. I had to leave with a tourist group to Lebanon for six months for my job, and when I came back, Nadira had left. I found a letter, and the letter said that Nadira had been diagnosed with cancer. Also, after so long, she is finally expecting a baby. The shock made me numb for a week. I couldn't figure out what I should do! Then I realized that she can only return back to one place only. I immediately came back to Vietnam, but didn't find her until after three months later when I was standing before her tombstone. I inquired all about her last days and came to hear the news I was searching for. She had given birth to a baby girl before her death. I ran to the hospital where she was born, but an European couple, childless, had taken her back with them. They gave me an address in Istanbul. I immediately left Vietnam and went to Istanbul. But I didn't find them. I stayed there for five years searching but no, I didn't find them. Perhaps they left Istanbul. A country gradually becoming disturbed by then. I gave up all hopes of finding my daughter and started looking for job as I was almost bankrupt with all the travelling and staying abroad. I went back to Europe, but can no more settle there. My heart wanted to come back to that place where it all began. I came back to India. I was staying at a Pondicherry post office for some months serving the Auroville Ashram when one day, came a letter. There was one line written.

'I just want to meet you once, Papa. I am coming to India. I will be in Kerala in the backwaters.'

At once I booked a ticket for Alleppy, to reach there three days before she would come. But she never came. I waited for a year there in Alleppy. There was no sign of her. In this world of social media it is not too difficult to find a man. Especially me, a solo traveller who, for money, often makes tours. Even in this age. Now it is over. I feel like I will never meet my daughter. I am bankrupt, destroyed, and moreover, my body is giving up. I wanted to tell someone my story-a cursed story of a cursed life. I took the train to the very beach where I found myself. Strangely, you came today. A man is not to end always uncontent. I believed that. I found you today. I told you everything today. That's it."

I sat there, speechless. The moon is still high in the sky but the wind is picking up and the sea rough. Some lightning sparked near the horizon.

Altamiro smiled.

"A storm is coming. Just the right time."

He looked tired.

"How long will you be here?", I asked him.

"Not for long. The waves know that."

"Perhaps I can help you in finding your daughter? Shall I come with you?"

"It is too late my son. Too late."

He stood, kissed my forehead, took the beer bottle and dumped it on the garbage can, then went inside.

The music from the instrument shop has stopped now. The shop is closed. The beach is silent now. Strangely silent. Only the sea roaring and the winds blowing. Almost in a mood of plunder. The moon is vanished. It's started raining. The blinking green lights of the trollers can no longer be seen. Only the crushing of the white waves on a desolate, empty beach. Suddenly, I can recognize the place. It is still a virgin, unknown beach. It is still primitive, mapless, and very much mine. The long gap of twenty years has vanished and it is me and the old sea again.

The rain came in no time.

The first blow of the storm hit the earth.

I started running towards my hotel.

That night the storm didn't stop. Each time I woke I found the earth shaking, the glass of the window, rambling. Yet, a silence prevailed, in spite of all the rampage, and there I find a refuge again, like I did in my first youth.

The next morning after breakfast, I walked to the shop where I found Altamiro.

But he was not there.

The Keralite lady, almost in tears, said, "Around three in the morning, I found him walking through the gate towards the sea within a ferocious storm. Then a boatman found him jumping on the waves and that was the last time he was seen."

I rushed into his room without asking the lady.

As far as I know he should have written something.

But no, there is nothing.

No there is.

Something.

A letter covered with a paperweight.

A letter from a woman.

'Papa, I am in Syria, in Damascus. I know I cannot meet you now. I have to do something for these merciless killings. At least I will try to save some life. I never saw my mother, but I have seen you, hearing about you from many people who have seen you. Perhaps one day when we can meet, you would tell me the reason why you, the person who travelled the world, never came to see me, his own daughter.

More than my father you are still my hero.

I am the daughter of that hero.

I love you Papa,

Zina.'

I looked upwards towards the sea.

The last word of Altamiro came to me.

'A storm is coming. Perhaps it is the right time.'

I cannot deny the truth that, perhaps, truly, it was the right time.

For a man to go.

Friction
Veronica Haunani Fitzhugh

There was once a box with rose colored powder sand and blue neon sides called Escafe. One day a boy and a girl sat side by side parallel playing at making sand castles. The castles were shaped from similar buckets and mixtures of sand and water and architectural leanings. Yet, the boy's castles' foundations hovered about a foot above the ground.

The girl noticed the extra height and thought it wonderful.

She reached her hands into her foundation and lifted. The foundation began to slip through her fingers.

She remembered how the sun pushed through the gaps of her fingers as she covered her flushed face mourning the loss of her grandmother. She remembered the water rushing through her fingers when she left all she had known to escape the flood that would take all she had known and leave in its wake smells of madness, tastes of bile, and shards of memories poking the edges of her mind. She remembered tracing the edges of fences around new homes with strangers. She remembered the door closing behind her after she told them her truth.

Her castle was ruined.

She overcame her shyness and asked the boy if she could live in his floating castle.

He told her no. His castles were homes for his thoughts and books and calculators.

"But, I can teach you how to build your own floating fortress. Forget the illusion that teathers you to the ground. Build your castle in the air instead of attempting to raise those caught in their gravity. Be free of ties and lies. Be free."

She took a deep breath and released herself from her entanglements and discovered she did not need high heels or even boys with rising castles to soar. Underneath the braids of modernity, she found delicate, ancient, raven black wings that carried her toward the loving sun of her smiles and other adventures.

The Derringer Doll

Bill Engleson

I took the Evening Express out to the valley. Hadn't been there in years. The rolling expanse of farmland that I remembered from weekend excursions with family and friends a lifetime ago was mostly gone, much of it plowed under, replaced by endless rows of tract housing and storage warehouses.

And a few prisons. You can never have enough prisons.

It was hump Wednesday. The Express was chock-full of work-weary passengers of all ages. Some looked like they wouldn't survive the balance of the week. A few seemed so long in the tooth that, arguably, they might be better off rocking in the breeze on the porch of the Happy Pines Retirement Home. If they could afford it. More and more I was seeing the elders of our country forced to claw their way back into an increasingly competitive, ravenous workforce.

My girl, Sheila, had taken a call earlier in the day from Frank Colfax. His wife, Sally Colfax, had been missing for a day. He hadn't notified the cops. Sheila didn't ask why no police report. She knew about runaway wives. She was even considering doing a runner herself.

Colfax met me at Buxton Station. It was like looking in a mirror. Bearded, lanky, belly curving into a pot, he wore his seventy five years as if each of those years had been shrouded with progressively more sorrow.

"You're older than I thought you'd be," he said.

"I'm older than I thought I'd be, too," I ricocheted back.

He cracked a perfunctory smile. The effort seemed to pain him. Maybe he was out of practice.

We walked over to a small diner, grabbed a corner table, ordered coffee and pie and huddled.

Once the waitress departed, Colfax got down to it. "Swan McGarvie says you're…you were… *exceptionally* discreet. Are you?"

"So, Swan referred me?"

"Yeah. That a problem?"

"No. No it isn't. It just…I haven't given much thought to him in years. I'm astonished that he's still alive."

"Really! Well, he is. In fact, he spoke as if you and he were as thick as…. well, close."

"We were never close." Now it was my turn to smile.

I had been a woefully reckless rookie on the Capital City Police Force. One damp Sunday I had my life altering collision with Swan McGarvie and his high energy, high profit, take no prisoners crew, the North Pacific Gang. That morning, I was on foot patrol. A skid road denizen had been viciously thumped for his half mickey of paint remover and George Dalton, my training officer and I'd chased the perp a few blocks over into the business district. At one point we split up and I blindly stumbled onto a heist crew exiting Regal Jewellers. One of the gang pulled a pistol, was about to seal my envelope with a bullet when another of the gang slapped it away. My saviour rushed up to me, breathed heavily into my face and said. "You owe me one, Laddie. What's your name?" Like a baby, I rattled off my particulars. Even gave him my phone number. He snatched my service revolver, bound my hands loosely and the gang took off.

Dalton found me in minutes, shook his head, untied me and said, "You tell the suits you lost your revolver on my watch, I'll finish you off myself."

That night, McGarvie called me at home. Could he drop over? And, he added, no, I didn't have a choice. It felt like I was sinking in quicksand. Come over, I said, imagining my life, my novice career, fizzling to a quick, tragic finale.

He came by as promised, returned my firearm, buddy punched me on my right shoulder, said, 'you won't regret this, Laddie,' and that was that. First he had saved my life and then my career. Overnight he became my underworld Rabbi.

I stayed on the force another two years. My ethics were shaky. I knew I was not cut from true blue cloth.

I became a P.I. Swan had a wide range of acquaintances. Many of these shadowy, wealthy, underworldly fellow-travellers became the source of much of my business.

Over time, my obligation to Swan diminished. I made my own bones. I knew the same people he knew. Years later, he retired to Costa Rica. My life was almost my own again.

"Well, close or not, Swan speaks fondly of you," Colfax brought me out of my reverie

I nodded and said, "Tell me about your wife. You have a current picture?"

"Yeah! My sweet Sal!" He reached into the inside pocket of his overcoat, withdrew a snapshot and handed it to me. Her face was haggard, the skin seemed as dry, as wrinkled as a bad plaster job. Her eyes stared down, as if the notion of looking in the lens of the camera was too much to manage. "She…" he was struggling to say something I assumed he had not ever fully accepted, "Sal was a vibrant woman once. Fifteen years younger than me. Smarter, too. Smart as a whip. Alive, eh! And then, her mind, well, this is how I think of it, her brain got slowly gobbled away."

"Dementia?" I offered the obvious guess.

"Yeah. Early onset. Very early."

"Then," I said, "She could be out there wandering in traffic or the bush. It's a good reason to notify the authorities."

"There's more to it. The last couple of weeks, Sal was starting to seem… like the old Sal. Memories I'm sure she hadn't had in years started to… percolate."

"So, that was good! Right?"

"Except…look, this stays between us, right?"

I reassured Colfax yet again. "Absolutely!"

He then pulled out a magazine from his overcoat pocket. It was a copy of Crime Gazette, one of a number of True Crime Magazines popular pre-internet. "It's the June, 2005 edition. You familiar with the sort of content these magazines have?" he asked.

"Mostly crap and speculation," I offered my two-bits worth. "What's the significance?"

He turned the cover towards me. It was a striking image. A beautiful naked blonde model, hair curling like a windswept row of ripe field corn, lounging in a white claw-foot tub, a half-smoked cigarette dangling from her lips, smoke swirling cloud-like, a derringer dangling, being fondled in the long, slick, smooth fingers of her left hand. The type screamed out WHATEVER HAPPENED TO THE DEADLY DERRINGER DOLL?

"Have you heard of the Derringer Doll?" Colfax asked.

I took a dip in my shallow pool of memory. "Some mysterious hit lady? Going back a few decades if it is."

"Sally," he declared.

"Your missing wife is the Derringer Doll?"

"Was. Is. Sally's mind has been lost for almost twenty years. Ten years ago, I picked up this magazine, brought it home, thinking, maybe it might mean something to her. I mean, the picture is of some model…doesn't really look like she did. But it didn't do a thing. Anyway, two weeks ago, she was rummaging around on our bookshelf and found it. I can't explain it but she stood there for quite a while, holding the magazine, staring at it and then she said, 'this is about me, Frankie, isn't it?'"

I sipped some coffee, took an overdue mouthful of my lemon meringue pie, and rubbed my bearded chin thoughtfully. There was something about the magazine picture that stirred me…

"So you think the magazine cover sparked some recollection for her this time."

"She kept gawking at it. Two nights ago, in bed, she woke me up and said…'one last hit, Frankie. One last hit.' In the morning she was gone."

"Do you know what she meant?"

"Oh, yes. There was one contract she hadn't completed…because of…her condition. I think she's finally remembered that debt. Sal had a tremendous work ethic."

"Who was she supposed to…kill?"

"That's the thing. Her contract was cancelled. The deposit returned. A change of heart. Rarely happened."

"Who was it? Is there any way she could still get to…her target?"

He looked sheepish, green around the proverbial gills. He'd ordered a slice of apple pie earlier. Maybe it had been off.

"*You* were the target," he blurted out.

"Me? *ME*?" That was unexpected. "Who'd want…?"

"Swan McGarvie. He was cleaning house. But he changed his mind."

"After your wife began to lose hers…" I exclaimed.

"Well, yeah, and…here is how she looked back then," he said, handing me a Polaroid. Ring any bells?"

I clutched the photo. A long-ago memory…an improbable night, Sunday, July 16th, 1995, came floating back. There had been a mini-heatwave. I arrived home late. After dark. The last thing I expected was a stark-naked blonde beating the heat in my tub. She'd cooed, "Swan asked me to drop by and give you a treat."

Sometime before morning, she dressed and departed. Strangest night of surprizes I ever had.

"I'm confused," I told Colfax.

"Well," he said, "My Derringer Doll is out there looking for you. Swan thinks that'll motivate you."

McGarvie was so right!

Motivation was ravaging me.

I'd get right on it.

Bill Engleson is a Canadian author and retired child protection social worker. He was born in Powell River, BC, raised in Nanaimo, and spent his first year of life trapped aboard his parents leaky fishboat. He resided in New Westminster for most of his adult years, retiring to Denman Island in 2004.

He writes long fiction, flash fiction, essays, poetry, letters to the editor, and, of late, book reviews for the Ormsby Review, an online journal about B.C history and literature.

He has been writing most of his life. His first couple of efforts, poetic in nature, were printed in his mid-teens (quite a long time ago) in the, now, sadly defunct Nanaimo Daily Free Press.

He self-published his first novel, *Like a Child to Home,* in 2013. The novel tells the story of social worker, Wally Rose, and the world of child protection.

Silver Bow Publishing released his second book, a collection of humorous literary essays titled *Confessions of an Inadvertently Gentrifying Soul,* in October, 2016.

Additionally, he has had flash stories published in Indies Unlimited 2016 Editors Choice Flash Fiction anthology and the recent Centum Press anthologies, One Hundred Voices Volumes One and Two.

He is working furiously, in between moments of sloth, on several new projects, including a prequel to his first novel entitled *Drawn Towards the Sun*, a mystery, *Bloodhound Days,* and a convoluted collection of home-grown, satirically tinged essays, *DIRA Diary: Tall Tales of Democracy in Traction.*

His website/blog is www.engleson.ca

Above Ground

Niles Reddick

Polly didn't feel like going into Wal-Mart at midnight and working until eight in the morning. Her feet were hurting from all the walking she'd done at the farmer's market, grocery store, and mall, seemingly an every other week cycle she put herself through, and when she became bored with it, she changed it up a bit by switching stores, the order of her visits, varying the times she visited, or changing the route she took. She needed the Wal-Mart money to pay her bills, and in the middle of trying to survive, she was also working on her registered nurse's degree at the community college.

Polly was fortunate and blessed to be the recipient of a scholarship, so she was going tuition free. Most people, in fact, had the opportunity in Tennessee to go to college tuition free. This was something the progressive mayor of Knoxville turned Governor---Haslam---had set in policy, and it had worked. Tennessee lead the way in the nation on federal financial aid application submission and even President Obama had come to Tennessee to talk about this program to the nation. Polly had liked Obama, not because his own father was from Africa like she was, but because he had a way of speaking that people liked. She didn't think he had been the best president, but then, she didn't think any of the modern ones had been. Of course, she did believe that good and bad were determined many years after they left office, so time would tell. Polly said that a lot: "Time will tell."

She'd said it a lot to Maxine, a slim black and feisty female who worked at Wal-Mart and had become a friend to Polly. When Maxine talked about her own children and what they might or might not do in life, Maxine had told Polly, "I told 'em to take they problems to the Lord ever chance they got cause you don't know if you got tomorrow, but when you wake up and you above ground, honey, it's a blessin'." Polly liked Maxine even though she knew Maxine was a bit off kilter, particularly when she started talking about "the helicopters."

Maxine apparently believed that the helicopters, not just from the regional hospital, but the state patrol office, were coming over her neighborhood and spraying people. "It's that Agent Orange is what it is. They killed all them people in Viet Nam and now they killing us black folks." No amount of "Now, Miss Maxine, I think those helicopters are trying to help people, working wrecks on I-40, and getting people to the hospital quickly, or going after criminals" could convince her. Maxine would respond, "Baby, now I know you'se come from Africa and was raised by white folks, but it's different here, and you got to understand. They see you as black. When you start talkin', they know you from somewhere else, but you can't trust 'em. You see them helicopters comin', you get in the house. I know people thanks I'm crazy, but I done seen it."

Polly stood in her bedroom, glanced at herself in the floor-length mirror. Her hair was slick and pulled back into a ball. She had puffy eyes. They looked as if they were water balloons, the fluid moving somewhere else when she pressed on them and then returning when she didn't. Her Wal-Mart shirt, her name stitched in cursive that most students didn't understand because cursive was no longer taught, was cleaned and pressed and tucked neatly into her jeans. After all, she took pride in looking the best she could, even if it was working at Wal-Mart, a place she had come to believe was illusion turned to disillusion.

It was an illusion to her because she thought it a representation of America, a place that had everything the world could offer, that offered people good deals, was fair and honest and built from the ground up by

Sam Walton, and perhaps at one time in history, this was an accurate vision.

Now, however, it had become the corporate giant that cornered the market, buying in bulk, so it could sell products at lower prices. Small businesses had evaporated, vacating downtowns like ghost towns of the West. Many of the products were imported and broke easily because they were made of plastic, and the people had been hypnotized by the bouncing yellow smiley face that talked of rolled back prices while hearing patriotic songs of an American past. In reality, prices weren't much cheaper than competitors and because so much was bought in bulk, many of the products had outlived their shelf lives, but people continued to come flowing through the electric doors, like endless waves on a beach. They loaded buggies, unloaded them in the self-checkout sections that had grown with a need to alleviate the pressure of the number of part time employees to maximize profit, they reloaded their buggies to push them to their vehicles, unloaded the buggies again before they drove home to unload a final time. All of this exercise was not decreasing the weight in America either. Polly's time there had created a state of disillusion, and she longed for the day she finished her RN degree and could divorce Sam Walton's legacy altogether. She actually believed if he were alive today, he would divorce himself from it, too.

Polly's adoptive parents, Jasper and Corrie Brown, had taught her to help others, to witness to everyone, to live simply and frugally. When they died in a car wreck in their sixties, they literally had nothing but the clothes on their backs. The doe had bolted out in front of them, they'd swerved to miss hitting her, and the car flipped, and had slammed into a culvert upside down. One of their friends had hypothesized that the deer was actually an angel sent to bring them home. There had been no fan-fair funeral, just a simple service with some friends attending in addition to Polly, and none of their friends had offered to help Polly or be there for her. Polly didn't understand that at all; in fact, she assumed they would be of more help to her. She wondered if it was because she was black, that she was from Africa, or that her parents were seen as outstanding models of Christianity and their friends were not the models they seemed to exhibit. She didn't know why, but she knew she was on her own at eighteen and would likely have to go to work full time once she graduated high school. Polly didn't even have the funds to pay for the funerals, but the co-owners of the funeral home, the Knox brothers, let her pay it on time, with no interest added. Polly had opted for the least amount---no visitation, just a graveside preacher with pine boxes and small metal markers.

Even after the friends had blessed her and the minister had tried to be of comfort, Polly stood in the city cemetery with all its crypts and monuments---logs for the Woodmen of the World, white granite crosses for veterans, concrete cherubs for children---and she wept, not for her adoptive parents, but for herself. She'd become a citizen and lived in America for five years, since she was thirteen, and all that time had attended public school. She knew she should not be in the cemetery alone by herself, a place where drug deals went down on a regular basis, a place where acts of prostitution took place on marble slabs in the middle of the night for fifty dollars. In fact, Miss Ollie who'd run the largest house of ill repute in her day was buried in the cemetery, though her tombstone name read Harriet. Polly had heard that in school from boys talking about it when the teacher left the room, planning to go there in the night for some foolishness or another. She thought boys were dumb for the most part, or at least that is how they seemed to her in high school.

"Hey baby, got a smoke?"

Polly hadn't seen the man approach, but she surmised he'd been watching the service from behind one of the crypts covered by shadows of the red maples.

"I don't smoke."

"Loan an old man a dollar?" He grinned, showing only a few teeth, a life somehow lost along the way.

"Don't have a dollar, but I can talk to you about God."

"Bitch, you'se crazy. God ain't done shit for me." The homeless man sauntered off, his faded and stained khakis about four sizes too big and sagging just enough to be in style with some of the younger boys in town had he been their age.

"It's not about what God can do for you, but what you can do for God." Polly cupped her hand and yelled after him, but the old man had kept going. She hadn't been afraid, but realized she should move on. In the fall, the sun set even earlier, and she knew she should not be in the cemetery come dark. Nodding goodbye to her adoptive parents, Polly had climbed in her used car, an old tan-colored Altima she used to get to school, home, work, and church.

She'd kept thinking about being alone. Polly knew she'd come into the world alone and would leave the world alone, and she had been raised in a Christian tradition in her hometown of Askum, Ethiopia, a place that had received worldwide attention because it was purportedly the resting place of the Ark of the Covenant, held in a small church and guarded twenty-four hours a day. Not even the head of the Christian church of Ethiopia had seen it---only the one who was chosen by all priests for purity was to guard and protect it until death had been inside to see it and no one had certainly looked inside it, where it was believed to hold the tablets revealing the ten commandments, Aaron's rod, and manna from heaven. Duplicate arks had been fashioned and placed in all Christian orthodox churches, and Polly believed the ark was a symbol of power and of history (it had been in Ethiopia for many years, since Sheba's son Menelik, by King Soloman, had it taken there after the collapse of Jerusalem). Polly's maternal grandmother told her when she was small she was a direct descendent of Solomon and one day she would be brought to greatness because of this.

Polly wanted to believe her grandmother, but that was very difficult given circumstances life brought her way. Plus, she had heard too many Americans trying to connect themselves to historically important or wealthy people just in the few years she'd been in country. It amused her to hear those stories, too, because she knew if just limited people she'd known in high school who thought they were descended from royalty or historically important people, and she extended that view to the same percentage of students in all American high schools, then the total number who asserted they were descended from royalty or historically important people would exceed what might be mathematically possible. Clearly, she believed that Americans had a deep need to cling to a belief in something greater than poverty and lower class roots, which is from what most of civilization descended.

Polly was eight when her own mother had died of AIDS in Ethiopia, and Polly's father gave up the coffee work at the farm and went to Kenya in search of work. He had the AIDS virus as well, and within a year, he had shriveled to skin stretched over a skeleton and died. Polly's two siblings had stayed behind with her paternal grandparents in Ethiopia to continue work on the coffee farm, and Polly went to live with an aunt and uncle in Uganda. She had been too young to help financially in the family. Later when her aunt and uncle could not care for her, they took her to the orphanage in care of Jeremiah and Rebecca. They'd comforted Polly on the loss of her parents, on the rejection she felt from her own family, and it wasn't until the Christian missionaries from America expressed interest in adopting Polly that Polly had begun to feel wanted again.

Polly and her parents had been living in a small clapboard house next to Mt. Zion church, where Mama Corrie played the piano in exchange for rent, and where Papa Jasper helped the preacher, a friend they'd met on a mission trip some years prior. Polly had stayed on in the house for three months, until graduation, making ends meet as best she could waiting tables and had been thrilled when Wal-Mart called her for an interview. Though it hadn't been a full time offer, the pay was decent. The only full time employees at Wal-Mart were the management and they had benefits; the part time employees had no benefits, except what they might get through the government, but Polly was young, didn't need anything much.

When Polly had gone by to make a payment on Mama Corrie and Papa Jasper's services, the Knox brothers told her about a garage apartment behind Professor Bray's near the private university in an older, but good, part of mid-town. It had occurred to Polly at the time that it was folks like the Knox brothers that made Jackson special---families who had made their lives here, who were always helping other people in small ways, when it wasn't required.

She was excited about graduation and she wished Mama Corrie and Papa Jasper would be there to celebrate with her. Polly vowed she'd make her own pound cake to celebrate. That's what Mama Corrie always made and her cakes had always been moist and almost melted in her mouth. She missed them. She thought she might invite Maxine, but the school had planned for a helicopter to come and drop blue and gray balloons, school colors, on the graduates. Polly thought that might send Maxine over the edge.

Polly changed her focus from the mirror and folded her pajamas and placed them on the edge of her double bed. She opened the venetian blind in the bedroom to let a little light inside and walked into her living room, turned off the flat screen TV (a deal she'd found at Wal-Mart), and made sure her coffee pot was unplugged, a habit she'd been grilled on by Mama Corrie. She loved coffee, almost as much as she liked the coffee she occasionally bought at Starbucks. She'd had a small BUNN coffee maker before, but it didn't last six months and despite the fact that it had a three-year warranty, they didn't return her emails when she queried them. She had not kept the receipt, so she didn't want to try to get a refund at Wal-Mart because she didn't want them to think she was up to something as an employee. They had several employees who had been caught stealing in one form or fashion and had been let go. It seemed the employees forgot there were cameras everywhere, except in bathroom stalls. She'd heard stories from Maxine about employees "hookin' up" in the bathroom on breaks. Polly was glad to be above ground, locked the dead bolt to her garage apartment, got in her Altima, and headed out.

Poor Farm
Niles Reddick

They found Oliver on one of the new benches in the reading park right next to the library. His bench faced the fountain. The waterfall in the cast iron fountain purchased by the library board was like Oliver---frozen. The EMT's got Oliver to the emergency room and then he was sent downstairs to the morgue, and it was almost an hour before his outstretched arms thawed and fell, banging the table and startling the attendant. Inside his coat pocket was a pint of Seagram's gin, always called knotty head by Oliver. The long wool coat that had been his cover smelled of urine, and the cloth tote bag that doubled as his pillow held a few snapshots of family, underwear, socks, another pair of jeans, and a flannel shirt.

Library staff had encouraged him to go to the shelter, get rid of the gin, if just for the night because of the raining ice and dangerous dip in temperatures, but he said he'd be alright. In fact, the shelter didn't open that night. The shelter rotated from church to church, and the mega church members who were supposed to host the shelter didn't think their 4x4 SUVs would make it on the ice. They left a voice mail at the soup kitchen that maybe the homeless people could just sleep at the kitchen after supper.

The library staff couldn't believe it when they found out Oliver had frozen, right out in the open with his arms reaching up toward heaven. They wondered who'd tell his family in town, the same family that had thrown him out too many times to count because of his stealing to buy more knotty head. They wondered who'd pay the funeral bill, if the community or state picked up the tab. They felt bad they didn't just let him in to sleep in the hall of the library. He wouldn't have stolen a book. No one stole books; they forgot to bring them back or didn't because they were lazy. It was against the policy to let people stay in the building after hours. If the police happened by, spotted him, and reported it, somebody's job would've been in jeopardy. Staff couldn't have taken him home. Besides, they didn't have room, and he might steal from them to buy alcohol.

The paper reported a few fragments, not quite a paragraph, about a vagrant drunk. Patrons told library staff it served him right, that he could have quit if he would have tried and that it wasn't *that* cold. A couple of older patrons said there should be a permanent shelter, like the one the county used to have. Known as the poor farm, the poor and destitute lived and pitched in with chores until they moved on or died and were buried in a pauper's cemetery. It made sense to the staff, but they knew it would take an activist or government leader to spearhead such a monumental effort.

Later in the afternoon, another homeless alcoholic fellow named Jordan came in and told the staff he'd slept in the afternoon and kept moving during the night to keep from freezing. He said about three in the morning the night Oliver died, he said he saw a young man who called himself Mike and who was also a Viet Nam vet hovering near the park. Mike told Jordan he'd been one of a dozen men Oliver had dragged back to a foxhole after they'd been shot or injured until medics could get them out by chopper. He watched Mike reach down to Oliver and help him up and out and thanked him for his service to others. Library staff figured Jordan was crazy from all the alcohol and would probably be next.

Niles Reddick is author of the novel Drifting too far from the Shore, a collection Road Kill Art and Other Oddities, and a novella Lead Me Home. His work has been featured in over a hundred and fifty literary magazines all over the world including Drunk Monkeys, Spelk, The Arkansas Review: a Journal of Delta Studies, The Dead Mule School of Southern Literature, Slice of Life, Faircloth Review, among many others. His new collection Reading the Coffee Grounds will debut in spring 2018.

His website is www.nilesreddick.com

AFTERGLOW
Glen Donaldson

It was an after dinner announcement no one had seen coming. After a great many years spent toying with the idea from the comfort of her upholstered recliner lounge chair with the polished wooden lever at the side, great grandmother Bertha Babcock had decided the time was finally right to get her very first spray tan.

It was now or never for the heavyset 88 year old, who, in her youth, had cut a svelte figure working at the local frog canning factory but via the passage of time, the birth of six children and one too many whoopee pies and Portuguese pastries had come these days to resemble more like one half of the popular bingo call for her age – "two fat ladies".

Bertha Babcock had devoted some time on the internet to checking out tanning salons before deciding on one called AFTERGLOW, about ten minutes drive from her house. In amongst her fact-finding research, which included reading numerous horror stories of spray tans gone wrong ('a radioactive orange colour which left the wearer smelling like vegetable oil for days' seemed to be a reoccurring complaint) she'd also managed somehow to take in the episode of the American sitcom FRIENDS where Ross is shown going into an automated tanning booth (like a carwash for humans) and due to a failure to pivot fast enough emerges with a half bronzed body.

But with the occasion of attending her granddaughter's upcoming wedding spurring her on to want to look her glowing best, Bertha was determined to ignore the stories of other's misadventures and forge ahead anyway. The person she'd spoken to on the phone at the salon had assured her she would be in capable and experienced hands.

The next morning her son Phillip arrived at the house in his silver grey Ford Bronco utility to pick her up and drive her to the salon. After the short journey during which Bertha again reminded Philip of her wish to have her ashes scattered at sea upon her death and her desire to visit the Crater of Diamonds State Park in Arkansas sometime prior to that happening, they pulled up in the car park of the salon and began the task of extracting Bertha from the front seat of the car. This took some minutes but eventually Bertha Babcock was on her way in, supported by her own cane walking stick and her dutiful, ever-patient son guiding and encouraging her with each step.

Inside, Bertha was at once hit with the sterile, over-air conditioned feel of a big box store and the slightly 'yeasty' aroma common to many tanning salons. She eased herself down onto the black leather waiting couch next to a laminated sign emblazoned in gold lettering with the words "We promise to do our best to make you look your best". Next, the twenty year old 'spray artist' girl walked through (Bertha thought she heard her introduce herself as 'Tiffany' but knew it might just as easily have been 'Tilly', 'Tina' or even 'Tigerlilly'). Even with her pasted on smile Bertha found her friendly and professional, but couldn't help wishing for a brief moment she was now facing someone more like Maude from her favourite retro show *The Golden Girls*. Bertha knew she wasn't going to enjoy having to get near naked in front of someone as young and bubbly as Tiffany, or whatever her name was.

After receiving her instructions on the poses to adopt while the 'fake bake' dark coffee chemical was applied, Bertha was handed a set of attractive nose plugs, a shower cap and a pair of too-tight green goggles and directed to walk down a tiled corridor into the 2nd room on the left that housed the stand up spray booth. The first thing she noticed once inside the room was how unbearably hot it was compared to the outside reception area. She looked up and noticed the sole ceiling fan wasn't moving. A moment later she realised why. A dead rodent was lodged in it, its legs dangling down toward Bertha. 'Tiffany' entered the room and explained in her best cheery tone that Bertha should change into the disposable underwear that lay on a corner benchtop and she would return in a few minutes when it would be time for the hoping-to-be- glamorous great granny to 'get her bronze on'.

After a 'respectful' time, the young salon worker knocked on the door and asked would it be all right to come in. "All ready my dear" was Bertha's buoyant reply. When 'Tiffany'pushed back the door she was greeted with a most unusual site. There was the great grandmother wearing the spray technician's surgical mask as underwear. She had somehow mistaken it for the g-string spanty that lay next to it. More incredibly she'd somehow managed to manoeuvre 'into' it. Spotting the girl's surprise but not knowing exactly what had warranted it, Bertha quickly switched to comedy mode and asked "Could you paint some tight ab muscles on me while you're at it?" The quip seemed to relax the young AFTERGLOW employee and she was able to complete the procedure in under ten minutes with Bertha emerging like a luminous Oompa Loompa ready to go to the wedding the next day.

On the way home from the salon with Philip driving however, there was one more sun-kissed moment of unintended pantomime. The Bronco utility was pulled over for a police random breath test. Phillip blew into the plastic nozzle offered to him by the officer wearing over-large mirror sunglasses. Though he was a non-drinker, the plastic metal device registered a reading for alcohol, though not enough to put him over the legal driving limit. He found out some time later it was the nearby powerful fumes from his mother's freshly spray tanned skin that had set off the machine and given a false reading for alcohol.

When the two arrived home, they sat down with the rest of the extended family in the living room. Everyone was eager to hear how Operation Tangerine Dream, as someone had dubbed it, had gone. Laughter and voices babbled happily like a flowing mountain stream for the next hour or so as Bertha Babcock held the floor like a fluff news reporter continually fed by the smiles and gentle gaze of those gathered. When Aunt Ophelia asked "Did they put it on with a paint roller?" the laughter echoed down the hallway and into each and every room of the house.

Soon it was time for the youngest children of the gathered clan to have their bath and as it was not her time to leave, great grandmother Bertha Babcock insisted on helping. The old bath tub was fashioned from tin and beaten into shape with a flat hammer. It was just big enough for a child to sit in and the water was never more than tepid. Before anyone could protest there was big bronzed Bertha, glowing radioactive orange by this time, arms deep in suds and bubbles scrubbing with a flat brush the grime from her grandchild Leroy's puppy fat bolstered five year old body.

When it was over, the entire house was treated to the genuinely horrible screams of bathetic Bertha reacting with all the grace of a wrecking ball to the sight of herself winding up with no tan at all halfway up her arms, making her look for all the world like she was wearing white gloves. And from a distance, at her granddaughter's garden wedding held in the city's Botanical Gardens the next day, that is exactly how it appeared. Unfortunately the super soak mishap also gave rise to a somewhat inebriated Uncle Spida, who was already slurring his words by the time the best man got up to give his speech, remarking on more than one occasion to anyone who would listen, how big Bertha's newly tanned look 'fit her like a glove'.

Glen Donaldson lists his three favourite words as (1) bugbear (2) Pollyanna and (3) shenanigator and admits to being fascinated why a group of squids isn't called a squad. He cites his all-time favourite movie as the Charles Bronson classic THE MECHANIC (1972) and never tires of popping bubble wrap.

Glen blogs at SCENIC WRITER'S SHACK.

Beautiful Idiots & Brilliant Lunatics
Victoria Kinnaird

"Oh, I love London society! It is entirely composed now of beautiful idiots and brilliant lunatics. Just what society should be." – Oscar Wilde

Attempt 1: The Dry Run

"How is it possible for your hair to go completely crazy in the ten minutes it takes you to drive to school?" Penny asked me, squinting through the late Spring sunshine.

I shrugged, rolling my shoulders like I could miraculously make my skin fit my slender frame after 17 years of terrible tailoring.

"I didn't do my hair this morning," I told her quietly.

Nope, instead of doing my hair, I'd sat on my creaky bed in my towel, water dripping down my back while I tried to figure out how to tell my best friend that I'm gay. So my white-blond hair had dried naturally, sticking out in a million different directions like I'd decided to stick a fork in the toaster instead of getting dressed in a timely manner.

"Lucas London, you know the rules!" she yelled, slapping my arm as we ambled through the school gates.

"I was busy," I replied, following her across the parking lot.

It looked like a normal morning on the face of it, my classmates milling about and trading whatever gossip they hadn't texted each other the night before. I got a glimpse of Will over by the gym, all boyish chestnut curls and a freshly pressed letterman jacket. He caught my eye, raising a hand in a stupidly adorable wave.

I resisted the urge to duck my head and blush. He was my friend, I had to at least try to maintain some semblance of normalcy. I waved back, earning a smile just as blinding as the morning sunshine.

I could practically hear Penny rolling her eyes.

"Penny," I whispered, curling my hand around her wrist.

"Lucas," she stage-whispered back at me, flicking her black fringe out of her eyes.

"I'm gay."

The whole world disappeared in a split second, like someone had flipped a switch. It was just me and Penny and the parking lot, the truth hanging between us like smoke.

My heart was in my throat and my stomach was making a valiant attempt to vacate my body through the soles of my feet. It had reached my ankles when her pretty face split into a beautiful, bright smile.

"Of course you are, Lucas."

Inhale.

Hold.

Exhale.

Wait.

What?

"Of course I am," I repeated, unable to supress the borderline manic laugh that was bubbling away in my chest.

"So...you gonna give me your calculus notes or..."

And that was it. I stared at her, stunned, not quite believing it had been so simple. Could it be that easy?

There was only one way to find out.

Attempt 2: The Queen Bee

Things going so well with Penny felt like a fluke. I'd convinced myself it couldn't be that easy. I shouldn't have been surprised that Penny was accepting of my sexuality – she was young, cool and had been in the school theatre programme way longer than I had.

But my mom? Well…she was going to be a whole different story.

I had my first asthma attack when I was 4 years old. I didn't remember it really, but my mom did. I could see the fear flickering in her gray-blue eyes every time I reached for my inhaler.

She'd been over protective ever since, not that I blamed her. It was just the two of us, always had been. In a lot of ways, she was all I had. The thought of changing our relationship, maybe damaging it beyond repair, made me sick to my stomach.

I showered, dressed and attempted to do my hair (didn't want to incur Penny's wrath) before heading downstairs for breakfast. I could hear her singing along to the radio from halfway up the stairs, smiling in spite of myself.

I hesitated in the doorway, wanting one more moment of normalcy before I changed (ruined?) everything.

She was fluttering about as usual, blond hair glittering as she spun her way across the kitchen, belting out some power ballad I vaguely recognised. The coffee had already gone cold and the eggs were burning, but it was perfect. I didn't want to change everything.

"Hey mom," I said, stepping into the kitchen. She beamed at me as I sat down, her expression darkening when I reached for my inhaler.

"Morning sweetie!" She chirped, forcing the worry away as she started covering our little scrubbed wooden table with plates of food.

"Why do you always cook so much food?" I asked, chuckling. It hadn't always been this way – I dimly recalled TV dinners and Pop Tarts twice a day, my mom hesitating in the line at the grocery store while doing some last-minute calculations.

"I like knowing you're not hungry," she replied with a delicate shrug before she poured out two mugs of black coffee.

"You keep feeding me like this and I'm never gonna get a boyfriend."

Inhale.

Hold.

Exhale.

It was out before I could stop it, the words tumbling from my mouth and spilling all over the table. I'd literally spent years planning this conversation, trying to figure out how to come out to my mom. There was a whole speech and everything.

"Well, if he's the right boy, he won't care," she said smoothly, picking up her iPad as if I hadn't said something so completely out of the blue. "And if this hypothetical boyfriend does care, he's not the right boy for you, Lucas."

"Mom," I began, voice cracking with the strain. I had no idea what to say or how to say it, but I had to say something, anything.

"Lucas," she smiled, her eyes glittering with unshed tears. "When you had your first asthma attack, I was so scared. I had no idea what was happening or how to get you through it. So I held you in my arms and told the universe that there was nothing I wouldn't do to keep you happy, healthy. I just wanted you to live. I would've given anything."

"But I pulled through," I reminded her. "I'm ok, Mom."

"I know," she nodded, tears finally spilling free. The skin around her eyes crinkled when she smiled. "I know you're gay. I've always known."

"You have?"

"And it doesn't change anything. All I want is for you to be happy. Are you happy?"

"I'm getting there," I murmured, shoulders straightening as I took a deep breath. "I'll get there."

Third Time's the Charm

Of all the people I wanted to tell, Will was the one I'd known for the least amount of time. So, logically, he'd be the one that meant the least, the one I shouldn't be worried about.

But my stomach didn't get the memo and my lungs had chosen to ignore it. I felt sick and breathless as I waited for him outside the gym. He'd agreed to help me paint sets after his basketball practice. He'd hit six foot at 13, I was pretty sure I'd been 5'5 since the day I hit puberty. It meant set painting wasn't really my strong suit.

Will was gracious about everything he'd been gifted with – his easy good looks, his athleticism, his nuclear family, his casual intelligence. It would've – should've – been easy to hate him if he wasn't so god damn nice about everything.

He strolled out of the gym, his hair slicked back and still damp from the shower. His gym bag was slung over one broad shoulder. I reached out for it unconsciously as the strap started slipping. Our fingertips brushed.

Inhale.

Hold.

Exhale.

"Hey," I said, smiling wide and genuine. "Good practice?"

"Not bad," he replied, falling into step beside me. "Everyone's working real hard. Last season together and everything."

The reminder that our last year at high school was slipping away hit me like a sucker punch, making my head spin. People like Will – gorgeous, well adjusted athletes – aren't friends with people like me in the "real world".

That was why I had to tell him, why I needed him to know the truth before he snapped up an athletic scholarship and disappeared into the life he was supposed to lead.

"We don't need to do this, you know," I muttered, searching his face for a hint of exhaustion. I didn't find one. "If you're tired."

"Hey, no," he grinned, bumping his shoulder against mine. "I promised. Plus, I like hanging out with you."

"Will?"

"Hmm?" He hummed, smiling up at the sky.

"I'm gay."

Inhale.

Hold.

Exhale.

"Oh, ok. Cool."

He didn't even break his stride, just kept walking towards the drama building like I hadn't just told him my deepest, darkest secret.

"Ok, you're the third person I've told and the third non-reaction," I sputtered, racing to keep up with him and his dumb long legs. "Did everyone know? Do I just look gay? Is it my eyebrows?" I demanded.

He laughed at that, a sweet easy laugh that fit in perfectly with the golden late afternoon sunshine. He was light and laughter and everything that was good in the world. I was crazy about him. Or just plain crazy. Whatever.

"What does "looking gay" even mean?" He asked, brown eyes shining when they met mine. "You don't look gay. Not enough glitter."

I laughed, stunned. It couldn't be that easy. I had friends online who'd put up with years of bullying, who'd been disowned by their parents. I knew people struggled every day. Why was I different? Why did I get to have this?

"It's not supposed to be this easy," I told him weakly, dizzy with the realisation that nothing was going to change, not really.

It wasn't like a weight had been lifted from my shoulders, it was like my strings had been cut. I just didn't know how to move on my own.

"Lucas," Will began, brows furrowing in the cutest way as he searched for the words. "This is part of who you are, right? And it always has been."

"Well yeah, but…"

"So if you've been gay this whole time, then you were gay when we started hanging out, right?"

"Yeah, but…"

"But nothing. You're Lucas London. You're the same guy now that you've always been – you just…you're more sure of it now. I'm happy for you."

"I guess?" I pushed my hair away from my face so I could look at him, really look at him. He was smiling down at me, eyes gone soft, so close I could smell his shampoo.

Inhale.

Hold.

Exhale.

Oh hell. I was more than a little in love with him, but…it was ok. I was ok.

"You should look into getting some glitter though," he grinned. "Now that you're out and proud an' all."

I stumbled after him, clumsy but moving forward, happy to follow him anywhere.

"Yeah," I agreed, brushing the backs of our hands together. "Maybe."

Victoria Kinnaird lives in Glasgow, Scotland with her French Bulldog, Charlie and her pug, Mr T. She graduated from the University of Strathclyde in 2009 with a Bachelor of the Arts degree in Journalism, Creative Writing and English Lit. Victoria has been writing since she was 15 years old. Her career in publishing began in 2013 with the release of *The Red Sun Rises*, the first novel in Victoria's LGBT YA paranormal romance series. In the years that have followed, Victoria has released three full length novels in *The Red Sun Rises* series and two novels in *The Keswick Chronicles*, her YA contemporary romance series. In 2017, Eren and Corbijn from *The Red Sun Rises* series won Chapter.Con's Most Loveable Couple fan voted award and were the only LGBT couple featured. When she's not writing, Victoria enjoys binging shows on Netflix, spending time with her family and going to the cinema. She also loves rock music, and most of her tattoos are related to bands that she loves!

Website link: www.victoriakinnaird.com

FRIENDS
(Another adventure with Bronte the cat & Cosmo the dog)
A quest to find real friends

Gino Gammaldi

One day, Cosmo and Bronte were talking about friends. They always thought they had a lot of friends, but realized they weren't sure what it meant to be a real friend. So, if they weren't sure what it meant to be a friend, they could not be sure who their friends really were.

"Do you know what a really good friend is?" Bronte asked Cosmo.

"Not really," replied Cosmo, "but, I think a really good friend would like me just the way I am."

"Yes, I like that," said Bronte.

"You know what I think?" Bronte went on. "I think that friends are people who are always there to help you when you need help."

"I think you're right," replied Cosmo.

"Maybe we should see who really are our friends." Cosmo said with excitement. "Let's go visit everyone we know and ask them."

"Yeah!" Bronte exclaimed. "Maybe we can also find out why they're our friends, then we will always know what it means to be a good friend. Doesn't this sound like a fun thing to do?"

"Sure does," said Cosmo.

"We should go to the town square garden first," said Bronte. "Mr. Fox is the gardener there."

"Good idea," replied Cosmo. "I think Mr. Fox is very nice. He has a kind heart. I trust he won't be too busy to be our friend."

Mr. Fox had a big, bushy, white beard and wore his hair in a ponytail.

"Hello, Mr. Fox!" cried Cosmo and Bronte as they ran towards him with excitement. "It's so good to see you again."

"We want to ask you something important," said Cosmo.

"Well, I'm always ready to listen if it's important," said Mr. Fox.

"Are you our friend, Mr. Fox?" they asked.

Mr. Fox was a bit surprised at this question.

"Of course I am," he replied with a chuckle. "Why do you ask?"

"Bronte and I think that it's very important to have real friends," Cosmo explained. "We just want to make sure we know who our really good friends are."

"We were also wondering how to know if someone is a really good friend," Bronte added.

Mr. Fox laughed and said, "Well, you are definitely right. Everyone needs good friends."

Mr. Fox looked at Bronte and Cosmo with a kind smile and said, "Friendship is one of the most important things in the world. A really good friend wants you to be happy and wants to help you if you are in trouble."

Cosmo and Bronte thanked Mr. Fox for being such a good friend.

"Do you remember Mrs. Rabbit?" Cosmo asked Bronte.

"Of course I do," Bronte exclaimed. "She's that nice lady who is always giving us yummy things to eat."

"Well, let's go visit her." Cosmo said cheerfully.

"Mr. Fox, would you like to come with us?"

"Well, it looks like I'm just about done with work today, so sure, I'll be happy to go with you."

When Mrs. Rabbit saw Cosmo and Bronte at her door, she immediately gave them a big hug. She even gave Mr. Fox a hug.

"Oh, it's so good to see you all," she said with a smile. "It's been such a long time since I last saw you."

"It's good to see you too, Mrs. Rabbit," Cosmo said.

"Oh my gosh! But why are you here," asked Mrs. Rabbit.

"Bronte and I want to find out who are our real friends," replied Cosmo.

Bronte looked up at Mrs. Rabbit and asked, "Are you our really good friend Mrs. Rabbit?"

"My dear, dear Cosmo and Bronte. You bet I am, you should not even have to ask. Let me tell you that a real good friend is someone who is happy to see you no matter how much time has passed since the last visit. Here are some yummy cakes I've just baked; you all must be so hungry."

Cosmo and Bronte decided to visit Mr. Squirrel and Mr. Wombat next. They lived deep in the forest. Mrs. Rabbit decided to go with them.

The woods were a bit scary, but, Cosmo and Bronte felt safe because they had each other and two really good friends with them.

Mr. Squirrel and Mr. Wombat saw them coming from down the track.

"Look, it's Cosmo and Bronte," said Mr. Squirrel.

"So it is," replied Mr. Wombat.

"It's so good to see you both, and who are these others that have come with you?"

"This is Mr. Fox and this is Mrs. Rabbit," replied Bronte proudly. They are our really good friends."

"Oh really," said Mr. Squirrel and Mr. Wombat. "Well, it's nice to meet you both."

"It was lovely to hear you say it is good to see us again," said Cosmo. "Does that mean you are both our really good friends as well?"

"Of course it does," replied Mr. Wombat. "We know how important it is to have really good friends, especially here in the forest. You never know when you might need help."

Just then, something delicate and colorful fluttered down onto Bronte's shoulder. It was Mrs. Butterfly.

"Hi!" she said. "I heard you were in the forest, so I thought I would try to find you; a big hello to you both."

"Hello, Mrs. Butterfly," said Bronte. "These are all of our really good friends. Will you please be our really good friend?"

"Well, I assure you that I too am your really good friend," she said. "Look, here comes Mrs. Sparrow. I happen to know she is also your really good friend."

Suddenly, they heard a noise from the nearby lake. Something big and green started to creep out of the murky water and make its way towards them. It was Mr. Crocodile and not far from him was Mrs. Tortoise.

"Hi everyone," they said. "What is all the noise and fuss we hear?"

"Oh! You surprised us!" said Mrs. Butterfly. "Cosmo and Bronte came to visit us! They want to make sure we are all their really good friends. Are you both their good friends?"

"Yes, I would like to think I am their really good friend," said Mr. Crocodile. "I don't have many friends. I think I scare them. But, they should not be scared because I won't hurt them."

"Look," said Mrs. Tortoise. "There's Mr. Wolf and Mr. Kangaroo. I bet they would like to be friends with all of us. It would be comforting to know I have some really good friends to look after me as I get older."

"Let's ask them," said Cosmo.

Before Cosmo and Bronte could ask, Mr. Kangaroo said, "We will always be your really good friends. I remember the time when you were both very helpful in solving a mystery in the town and got everyone to help each other. Anyone would want to be your friend."

Even Mr. Wolf, who normally just pretended to be very tough, said, "Well, you certainly are both very kind hearted. Everyone who has good friends or who has a family that loves them without condition should consider themselves to be very fortunate. I think that being your good friend would be good for me. I have a very important position in the village so I need all the good friends I can get."

All of the animals in the forest agreed with Mr. Wolf that it was very important to have good friends who love you no matter what. They came from all different parts of the forest. There was an owl, a tiger, an emu, a ram; even a cuddly, wooly lamb. It seemed everyone wanted to be friends with

Cosmo and Bronte.

But then, Mr. Bear, who had been sleeping, appeared. In a very loud and not so friendly voice he grumbled, "What is all this noise about? You have interrupted my sleep."

Then Mr. Tiger spoke.

"I know you are very tired and grumpy," he said in a comforting voice, "but you should really listen to what Cosmo and Bronte have to say."

"Very well then," Mr. Bear said with a grunt, "but make it quick."

"Excuse me for interrupting you, "Mr. Bear," said Cosmo. We're sorry for disturbing you. Bronte and I just want to find out who are our really good friends."

"Everyone here is a really good friend of ours," added Bronte.

"Would you like to be a really good friend to us, Mr. Bear?" Cosmo asked nervously.

Mr. Bear was a bit shocked. Most of the time the other animals were frightened of him as they were of Mr. Crocodile. He thought about all the times he could have used the help and comfort of a good friend.

"Yes, I would love to be your really good friend," replied Mr. Bear who didn't feel so grumpy and tired anymore.

Cosmo and Bronte were very pleased to have found out they had so many really good friends and what it meant to be a good friend.

They spent the rest of the day enjoying their friendships.

For more information on our Charitable Anthology Series, our authors, or our other books in this and other series, please visit :

www.snowleopardpublishing.com

and our

Owl's Nest Book Shop

www.ingramcontent.com/pod-product-compliance
Lightning Source LLC
Chambersburg PA
CBHW070600180626
46817CB00005B/1929